D1442927

real live boyfriends

by e. lockhart

RUBY OLIVER NOVELS
The Boyfriend List
The Boy Book
The Treasure Map of Boys
Real Live Boyfriends

Fly on the Wall
Dramarama
The Disreputable History of Frankie Landau-Banks
How to Be Bad (with Sarah Mlynowski and Lauren Myracle)

e. lockhart

real live boyfriends*

*yes, boyfriends, plural. if my life weren't complicated—
I wouldn't be Ruby Oliver.

a ruby oliver novel

delacorte press

Copyright © 2010 by E. Lockhart

All rights reserved. Published in the United States by Delacorte Press,
an imprint of Random House Children's Books, a division of
Random House, Inc., New York.

Delacorte Press is a registered trademark and
the colophon is a trademark of Random House, Inc.

Visit us on the Web! www.randomhouse.com/teens

Educators and librarians, for a variety of teaching tools,
visit us at www.randomhouse.com/teachers

Library of Congress Cataloging-in-Publication Data
Lockhart, E.
Real live boyfriends : yes, boyfriends, plural. if my life weren't complicated
I wouldn't be Ruby Oliver / E. Lockhart. – 1st ed.
p. cm.
Summary: Now a senior at her Seattle prep school, Ruby continues her
angst-filled days coping with the dilemmas of boyfriends, college
applications, her parents' squabbling, and realizing that her "deranged"
persona may no longer apply.
ISBN 978-0-385-73428-8 (hardcover) – ISBN 978-0-385-90438-4 (glb) –
ISBN 978-0-375-89758-0 (e-book)
[1. Self-perception–Fiction. 2. Dating (Social customs)–Fiction.
3. Interpersonal relations–Fiction. 4. High schools–Fiction.
5. Schools–Fiction. 6. Seattle (Wash.)–Fiction.] I. Title.
PZ7.L79757Re 2010
[Fic]–dc22
2009041988

The text of this book is set in 11-point Baskerville BE Regular.

Book design by Angela Carlino

Printed in the United States of America

10 9 8 7 6 5 4 3 2 1

First Edition

For Daniel

contents

real live boyfriends

1.

Real Live Boyfriends!

a definition:

A real live boyfriend does not contribute to your angst.

You do not wonder if he will call.

You do not wonder whether he will kiss you.

And he does not look at his phone while you are talking, to see if anyone has texted him.

Of course he calls. He's your boyfriend!

Of course there will be kissing. He's your boyfriend!

And of course he listens. He's your real live boyfriend!

You can sit down next to him at lunch whenever you want. There's no need for mental gyrations such as: Will he want me there when he's hanging with his friends?

Or will he half ignore me in order to seem golden in front of them?

Of course you can sit with him. He's your boyfriend!

You can assume you'll see him on the weekend. You can call him just to chat. You can expect he'll be nice to your friends.

Contrary to some rumors, however, you don't have to be in love. You don't have to engage in any horizontal action beyond what you're in the mood for. You don't even need to stay together after high school. But you have to like him and he has to like you—and everyone has to know you're together.

He's your real live boyfriend!

The Insanity of My Parents! And Romance!

from seventh grade to ninth, I had a real live boyfriend named Tommy Hazard.

Tommy was perfect. He had clear skin, he was never obnoxious in class, and he was excellent at sports. He had beautiful strong shoulders and a secret mysterious smile. Tall but not too tall. Great teeth. Smoldering eyes.

In fact, he was superhot and could have any girl he wanted. And the best thing was—he went weak whenever he saw me.

He was also imaginary.

I told my best friend, Kim, all about him. He changed according to my mood. Sometimes he was a surfer boy in board shorts and a bead choker, tossing the water out of his hair as he smiled down at me. Sometimes he was a skate punk. Other times a mod guy in a narrow tie who took beautiful black-and-white photographs.

Then I started going out with Jackson Clarke, sophomore year, and Tommy Hazard disappeared–I guess because I finally had a real live boyfriend with a real live heart pumping in his chest.

Only–then it turned out he didn't.

Have a heart.

And he didn't want to be my real live boyfriend anymore–

He wanted to be Kim's.

Flash to end of junior year.

When I wrote the above definition of a real live boyfriend, it was fourteen months since Kim and Jackson got together and shattered my heart, plunging me into an abyss of bad mental health. I wrote it sitting in the B&O Espresso, where Meghan and I were supposed to be studying for finals. We were hopped up on dobosh torte and coffee drinks, and I couldn't think any more about chemistry formulas.

I flipped to a new page in my notebook and wrote something else, just to give myself a break.

Meghan crinkled her sexy little freckled nose when she read it. "What do you mean, real live boyfriend?"

"Exactly what I wrote."

"But–" Meghan looked perplexed.

"What?"

"Isn't this just what a boyfriend *is*?" she asked. "Any boyfriend?"

Just to be clear, Meghan has had a pretty much continuous cycle of serious boyfriends since seventh grade. Me, I had been in the state of *Noboyfriend* since April of sophomore year, when the Kim/Jackson debacle made me pretty much dysfunctional.

And while you could argue that Meghan's male-oriented outlook on life was all about the fact that her dad died when she was twelve and that's why she's the only other teenager I know who sees a shrink on a regular basis, there was no denying that she was being truthful when she said she didn't know what I was writing about. She and her boyfriend, Finn, who was making espresso behind the counter at the B&O right that very minute, got together just before Spring Fling junior year and were as real and live as real and live could be. And before Finn, Meghan had been real and live with Bick.

And before Bick, with a guy she met at camp.

And before that, with Chet, who moved away.

And before that—you get the idea.

Meghan didn't know much about how it felt to wonder if a guy still liked you. She didn't know about half-boyfriends and awkwardness and partial breakups and all that human weirdness—partly, yes, because she is one of the most oblivious people I've ever met and really might not know human weirdness if it bit her, but also because she somehow knows how to connect with boys.

Not like they're Neanderthals or wildebeests or aliens or pod-robots, but like they're normal human beings.

Which obviously they are.

Only, it is extremely hard to tell sometimes.

"A real live boyfriend is more of a boyfriend than a lot of boyfriends," I told Meghan.

She took a sip of her mocha and shook her head. "If you were going out with a guy, why wouldn't you sit with him at lunch?"

I shrugged. "He might be having Dude Time."

"Dude Time?"

"You know, time with the guys. Time where they bond and don't want their girlfriends hanging on their arms."

"No," said Meghan decisively. "They get plenty of that at soccer practice. It is completely unacceptable to have Dude Time when your own girlfriend is in the actual room with you, eating tacos. What kind of guy would do that?"

"Lots of guys do that."

"What do they say?" asked Meghan. "Hey there, Roo, don't come near me at lunch today 'cause I'm hurtin' for some Dude Time?"

"No." I ate the last of my cake. "They don't call it Dude Time at all. That's what I'm calling it. They just give off a Dude Time feeling. Like they want you to leave them alone."

"That's dumb," said Meghan. "No normal guy would do that. You just had a bad experience with Jackson."

"No," I said. "I mean, yes."

"What's with this part?" Meghan wanted to know. She was rereading what I'd written. "'You do not wonder if he will call. You do not wonder whether he will kiss you.'"

I nodded. "Don't you ever wonder whether Finn will call?"

"No!" she laughed. "He calls me every morning before I leave for school and every night after dinner."

I sighed and yelled over to Finn, who was wearing an apron and reading Studs Terkel behind the counter, since the coffee shop was basically dead. "You're a real live boyfriend, Finn, you know that?"

He looked up. White skin, blond crew cut, big eyes. He's got nowhere near Meghan's level of sex appeal, but then, no one does. "I'm a what?" he called.

"Never mind," Meghan told him, giggling. "Roo just thinks you're nicer than most guys."

"I am," he said. "But she's only saying that 'cause I give her free cake."

"Okay," said Meghan, back to business. "But what is this here, about not kissing? If he's your boyfriend, wouldn't you be kissing all the time?"

"Only if he's your *real live* boyfriend," I said. "Not if he's a scamming mate[1] or a friend with benefits[2]

---

[1] Scamming mate: You fool around, but you don't hang out. Ever.
[2] Friend with benefits: You fool around, and you do hang out, but you are not *going* out.

or even a kind-of, sort-of, it's-all-very-confusing boy-friend.[3]"

"Ruby Oliver," said Meghan, "you are certifiable."

Yes. That, I thought—that's the trouble with me.

I am.

Because here's what I was really thinking about during that whole conversation:

Noel.

Asthmatic, funny, scrawny Noel. He of the combat boots and the cross-country runs, the painting classes and music magazines. Friends with everyone, best friends with no one, secretive, beautiful, witty Noel.

Long story short: I was crazy about him but he wasn't speaking to me. We'd had one amazing kissing extravaganza, then an atrocious misunderstanding late in junior year, the result of various complicated debacles partly involving the fact that my best friend Nora liked him first and he was therefore officially off-limits to me—and partly involving the other fact that in the eyes of most people at Tate Prep, I am a famous slut.

Noel, Noel, Noel.

It was insane to even be thinking of him.

●

I forgot that I had written all that stuff about real live boyfriends in my Chem notebook, and when my mother

---

[3] Kind-of, sort-of, it's-all-very-confusing boyfriend: Self-explanatory.

offered to quiz me on formulas for the final, I handed it over.

Mom was lying on the floor with her head on Polka-dot, our dog.[4] I was standing at the fridge feeling a wave of ennui because of the severe lack of deliciousness therein.

My mother was on a raw food diet.

We'd had salad for dinner, and our fridge contained two bunches of kale, celery juice, pickled carrots, peanuts soaking in water, and a number of other items too horrible to mention.

"Why don't we ever have dessert anymore?" I complained, shutting the fridge again. I don't know why I even bothered to open it. Just habit, I guess, left over from the days when there might have been pie or something chocolate in there. "Just for me and Dad, if you don't want to have it."

No answer.

"And don't tell me a banana makes a nice dessert," I went on.

"Can't you be supportive of the raw food way of life?" Mom said.

"I could if you didn't make me *live it with you.*"

9

---

4 Polka-dot is a harlequin Great Dane, spotted like a dalmatian. He is *not* a reasonable dog to have living with me, my mom and my dad in a tiny houseboat.

But then, nothing about my life is reasonable.

Mom ignored me. "Kevin, come look at this!" she called. Dad got up from his computer, where he was editing his garden catalog/newsletter, and bent over her shoulder. I figured she wanted him to decipher my writing on some part of the Chem notes.

"Did you read that, Kevin?" said my mother.

"Uh-huh."

"So?"

"So what about it?"

"So I'm not sure you're my real live boyfriend."

"I'm your husband," he said, kissing the top of her frizzy head.

"Ag!" I shouted. "Are you reading my personal things?" I stomped over and snatched the notebook out of her hand.

"Sure," Mom said, ignoring me and turning to Dad, "but I'm not sure you're my *real live boyfriend* because you don't always call me when you say you will."

"Elaine!" he moaned. "I forgot once last week when I was at Greg's playing Wii.[5] I wasn't even home late."

"No. You forgot that other time," she said accusingly. "When you said you'd call from the grocery store to talk about what we were having for dinner."

---

5 Greg is my dad's friend who has panic attacks so bad he never leaves his home. Which is completely what will happen to me if I don't get a handle on the panic badness that happens to me ever since the debacles of sophomore year. If you want to see Greg, you have to go over to his garbage-y, plant-filled apartment and bring him Chinese food. It is deeply pitiful.

Dad winced.

"I was sitting on the bench outside my yoga class," Mom went on, "waiting for you to call. Finally I gave up and went inside, but I missed all the chanting."

"You don't even like the chanting."

My mother coughed. "I'm learning to like it. Anyway, I was waiting for you to call and you never did."

"We've been married twenty years. I'm your real live boyfriend, okay? If that's what you want to call it." My dad went back to his desk in exasperation.

"Mom!" I waved my hand to get her attention. "Don't read my stuff. If it looks remotely personal, don't read it. Even if you're holding the notebook for some completely justifiable reason. It's not your business."

She held up her palm to silence me. "Ruby, not now. I'm talking to your father."

"It's hard enough to have any privacy living in this tiny houseboat without you reading my notebooks," I went on. This was something Doctor Z had suggested I do when the opportunity came up. To make very clear to my mother how I'd like to be treated and ask her to respect my privacy.

Only, Doctor Z has never tried to be clear with Elaine Oliver. Mom gave no indication whatsoever of having heard me.

"I don't know whether there's going to be kissing either," she complained to Dad. "Honestly. The other night I rubbed your neck and you didn't even turn around."

Ag, ag, ag and more ag.

"Oh, help me, Elaine. I was working under deadline. Are you trying to start an argument?" Dad barked.

"I'm expressing myself!" yelled Mom, leaping up from the floor. "You always want us to share our feelings, and now when I'm sharing my feelings you say I'm starting an argument! That's so unfair!"

Polka-dot hates when they argue, so he stood up and started barking. *Rouw! Rouw!*

"I'm your husband, Elaine!" yelled Dad. "I don't know why you're suddenly questioning everything!"

Rouw! Rouw!

"But are you my *boyfriend*?" Mom cried. "Ruby says the whole point of a real live boyfriend is that you can tell he's your boyfriend."

Rouw! Rouw!

"Ruby's in high school," Dad called over Polka. "Why are you listening to her?"

Rouw! Rouw!

"It's just how I feel!" stormed Mom. "Maybe because I haven't done a show in so long. Maybe because of what Juana said the other day." [Blah blah blah. Insert long monologue about her personal issues that's completely uninteresting to anyone under the age of forty-five]. "I don't know," she finished, nearly in tears. "I just can't tell! I can't tell if you're my boyfriend!"

Dad opened the door to our houseboat and called out into the night. "I am Elaine Oliver's real live boyfriend! I want everyone to know! My name is Kevin! I

am a gardener of rare blooms! I am her boyfriend forever and ever!"

Rouw! Rouw!

Dad kept yelling. "I'm telling *you*, Seattle! Elaine
Oliver is my woman!"

Mom started laughing. "You'll wake the neighbors."
She wiped her nose with a tissue.

Dad started singing, off-key but loud:

"I don't wanna sleep,
I just wanna keep
On lovin' you. . . ."[6]

"Okay, okay!" Mom cried.

"Don't you love Speedwagon?"

"Kevin!"

"I know all the lyrics. I can sing it from the begin-
ning."

She shook her head. "Not necessary."

"You want me to stop now?" Dad asked.

She nodded.

"You believe I'm your real live boyfriend?"

She nodded again.

Dad walked over and gave her a hug. Polka-dot
made a dash for the door and galloped the length of our
dock, which he loves to do at every opportunity.

---

[6] **"Keep On Loving You": Retro power ballad by REO Speedwagon. Dad is obsessed with retro metal. I think it makes him feel like he's still seventeen.
Though why anyone would *want* to feel like they're seventeen I have no idea.**

"Ruby, go collect the dog," Dad said, his face buried in Mom's hair.

When I got back the two of them were kissing.

Ag.

I am sure it's obvious why I need therapy.

A week after Dad serenaded the neighborhood, Noel DuBoise suddenly baked me chocolate croissants and wrote me a letter.

An apology.

An explanation.

Not a love letter, really. But a perfect letter.

All the badness between us washed away, and what I had been insane to wish for—insane to even think about—became a reality.

Noel and I were together.

He kissed me and sat with me at lunch and listened to me without checking his texts. Wrote me e-mails and called me and made me laugh.

Noel DuBoise was my real, live boyfriend.

An e-mail from early in the summer:

Hi Roo.

Tomorrow, your presence is requested at a meeting of the Mutual Admiration Society. Time: 4 p.m. Location: the Harvard Exit movie theater.

Do not go online and check what they are playing. Show up with faith in the Society's good intentions and taste in cinematic entertainment.

Also: bring Fruit Roll-Ups and Toblerone. The Society's only other member will bring drinks and spring for popcorn and movie tickets.

Confirm your attendance at your earliest convenience.

Noel

Another e-mail:

Roo,

I just dropped you off and came home to find the house dark. Parents asleep, little girls asleep, everyone in bed before my curfew.

I banged on Mom's door so she knew I was home, then climbed out on the porch roof outside my bedroom window. Tried to stealth it down the rose trellis. Figured I'd sneak back out and see you again because: all of a sudden I missed you like a complete sap. Even though I just saw you.

Planned the grand romantic gesture.

Nearly died trying to climb down rose trellis.

Really. Nearly died.

Seriously.

Okay, didn't nearly die. But did scrape my arm on some thorns.

The need for Band-Aids trumped my plan to sneak up to your bedroom window and throw pebbles until you saw me standing there in the moonlight.

Grand romantic gesture crashes and burns.

Bright side: I did use the bacon Band-Aids you got me. There are three on my arm with actual blood soaking through.

In the moonlight,

Noel

15

Even though I know there is no such thing as a happy ending[7], a little part of me thought I had found one.

Even though some people hated Noel and me being together.

Even though having a real live boyfriend didn't solve my mental problems or fix my family.

Even though life wasn't a movie.

It still *felt* like a happy ending. It did.

Until eight weeks later.

---

[7] You can't have an ending. It's impossible. Because unlike in the movies, life goes on. You're never at the end until you die.

3.

Panic Attacks and Rabbit Fever!

an unedited video clip:

Blurry images. Green stuff. Flowers. The focus locks on a very small greenhouse filled with rare blooms grown in containers.

Outside the glass walls, a warm July drizzle over the lake.

Inside, Roo and Noel sit together on a wooden crate too small to hold both their butts.

Roo wears her new rhinestone-studded glasses and a T-shirt of Noel's that reads DEATH: OUR NATION'S NUM-BER ONE KILLER. The gap between her two front teeth keeps showing because she's smiling so much. Noel's hair has too much gel in it and his arms look scrawny. His eyes are laughing.

Roo: The inauguration of my digital video camera.

Noel: (doesn't say anything; looks at his hands)

Roo: I bought it this morning with money I made mucking out stalls at the zoo and selling Birkenstocks to people with disgusting feet.

Noel: (stares like a deer at the camera)

Roo: (turning) Are you going to say something?

Noel: I feel dumb. The camera makes everything seem fake, suddenly.

Roo: I feel dumb too. But let's shoot some footage so I can practice editing.

Noel: Okay.

Roo: Just get past the dumb.

Noel: You got it.

Roo: Today is July eighteenth, I think. We're sitting in my dad's greenhouse and . . .

Noel: (starts kissing Roo on the neck)

Roo: (laughing) What are you doing?

Noel: You said ignore the dumb.

Roo: Yeah, but–

Noel: And you said you wanted to practice editing.

Roo: So?

Noel: (still kissing) So I'm ignoring the dumb and giving you something to edit out.

I spent a lot of time at Noel's place that summer. He lived with his mom and stepdad in a Victorian-style house in Madrona. He had two little half sisters and his folks were always around, cooking or scolding or complaining about the clutter. It was a nice place to be. Mrs. DuBoise told me flat out I could stay for dinner any night I wanted.

Noel didn't have a summer job[1], but he was expected to take charge of his little sisters two days a week. He'd bring them to the zoo while I was working for the landscape gardener there. They would bring spearmint jelly candies and feed them to me 'cause my hands would be covered in soil. Then when I got off work I'd take them to the Family Farm area and lift the little girls up to pet the llamas and feed the goats.

One day, when Noel went off to buy juice for us all, I helped the girls write notes on zoo stationery to Robespierre, my favorite pygmy goat. We stuck our letters in the bright blue box marked WRITE TO OUR FARM ANIMALS.

Dear Robespierre,

You are a nice goat. I did not know goats were so hairy as you. I thought you would have more like fur.

Love, Sydonie

Dear Robespierre,

Why am I not allowed to feed you my apple? I want to feed you my apple and see you eat it up.

From, Marie

---

[1] No summer job: Most of the kids who go to Tate Prep don't need jobs because their parents are loaded. I go there on scholarship.

Dear Robespierre,

That was my real live boyfriend, Noel!
Did you see him? Did you?

Don't be jealous. You are a pygmy goat and I am a human. It could never have progressed beyond ear scratching, you and me. Besides, you have Imelda and Mata Hari, both of whom obviously prefer you to that scraggly little pretender of a goat, Kaczynski.

When you write back, please tell me: Do you think it's all going to come crashing down? Do you think this is real life? Can I be this happy?

Love, Ruby

After my shift ended, Noel would usually drive me back to his place. I'd take a shower there and change into normal clothes.

Like I belonged in his house.

With him.

And it was just right.

I was in love.

In love. Yes.

It wasn't anything we said to each other, but it was how I felt.

And how I *thought* he felt.

I even told my shrink.

Just in case you haven't familiarized yourself with the painful chronicles of my high school career, I have a shrink because sophomore year—after Jackson broke my heart and Kim and all my other friends ditched me—I nearly went insane. I have managed to reach my senior year alive only because it turns out you can't *actually die* from embarrassment and misery. You just start having these awful, can't-breathe, heart-exploding episodes. Panic attacks.[2]

Now I have to go to therapy once a week.[3]

"*Love* is a big word," said Doctor Z when I told her about Noel. She popped a piece of Nicorette and waggled her Birkenstock off the end of her foot.

I played with the frayed hem of my jeans and didn't answer.

"This is the same Noel who hid his asthma from you, am I right?" she went on.

"Not his asthma. The fact that he hadn't been taking *care* of his asthma."

"And the same guy who wouldn't let you explain about the incident in the library? You two weren't speaking for a while?"

I sighed. "Same guy."

I hate it when Doctor Z asks questions that roundabout way. It's so shrinky-shrinky.

---

[2] Panic attacks: Episodes of heart palpitations and the feeling that there's just not enough air in the universe to fill my lungs.

    I sweat.

    I shake.

    It's just complete badness and I feel like I'm going to die every time it happens.

[3] P.S. About the panic attacks. If you get these too, you should tell your doctor to rule out any physical crap that might be going on. Then if it's only mental, the doctor can send you to the shrink.

What she really meant was: Do you honestly think this Noel is going to be a good boyfriend? Because he already has an iffy track record. And you, Ruby Oliver, can hardly afford to risk your precarious mental health for a guy who might turn out to be a jerk.

"It's the same guy who gave me his hoodie when my clothes got soaked in chemistry class," I told her. "Same guy who took me home from the Spring Fling when no one else would give me a ride. Same guy who made me a valentine. And baked me chocolate croissants. And said he knew all the gossip about me wasn't true."

Doctor Z didn't answer. She just blinked her big brown eyes at me.

"You're thinking I'm too defensive now," I said.

Again, no answer.

"Now you're thinking I'm getting all cranked over a silly high school thing, making it sound important, like some big romance, when in the larger scheme of my whole entire life, none of this will really matter," I said.

More silence.

"And you're gonna say I'm too boy-oriented, and I should be focusing on developing my friendships and not have Rabbit Fever all the time."[4]

---

[4] Rabbit Fever: My name for the kind of inadvertent sex mania I suffer from.

Like, sometimes I think about people undressed whom I would never, ever want to see undressed in real life. I mean, if I saw them undressed in real life I would run screaming from the room, either because they're way old and inappropriate (my swim coach, Mr. Wallace) or because they're deeply unattractive as human beings (Neanderthal Darcy), or both (the headmaster).

Doctor Z recrossed her legs and straightened her orange chenille poncho. But still, she said nothing.

"I've been in therapy a year and a half now," I told her. "I know how it works. I know what you're going to say before you say it."

"I'm not saying anything, Ruby."

"You're *thinking* it."

Doctor Z paused. "Maybe *you* are thinking it," she offered.

Here's Doctor Z: African American. Fortysomething. Seriously fashion-challenged to the point of wearing horrible crocheted ponchos and patchwork skirts. Cozy office in a generic office building. Mistress of the shrinky silence. Nicotine fiend.

Here's me: Caucasian. Nearly seventeen. Vintage dresses, fishnet stockings and Converse. Suffering from panic attacks and Rabbit Fever. Plus a general inability to relate to other human beings in a way that leads to happiness.

Here's what we have in common: We both wear glasses. We both live in Seattle. And we sit in this room together every week, discussing my problems.

Therapy is deeply weird. You talk and talk and someone else listens. This grown-up your parents pay money to, who has never met your friends, never been to your house, never seen your school—in other words, a person who's had no contact whatsoever with any of the things that are giving you angst.

You tell that person everything. And she listens.

"I ran into Nora the other day at Pagliacci's," I said, to change the subject.

"Oh?"

"Ever since I supposedly stole Noel from her, we just avoid one another. But two days ago I saw her and her brother getting pizza."

"Her brother Gideon?"

Doctor Z knows all about Gideon. He is superhot in a bohemian, necklace-wearing way, and I used to love him in sixth grade. Also, last spring his leg touched mine when we were watching a movie at Nora's house. And once, inexplicably, he came over to my house and helped me make doughnuts.

"That's the only brother she has," I said.

"What happened at Pagliacci's?"

"I was standing in line to pay for my pizza and the two of them came up behind me."

"Did you talk to them?"

"Gideon said hi. He's obviously ignorant that Nora now considers me a backstabbing, Noel-stealing slut. Or he pretended to be ignorant."

"What did Nora do?"

"She acted really, really interested in some Chap Stick she found in her bag."

"What did *you* do?" asked Doctor Z.

"I kept talking."

"What about?"

"Canned mushrooms: Are they a valid topping with a flavor of their own, like canned black olives? Or are they just rubbery disgustingness? Blah blah blah. Finally the guy in front of me paid, and I asked to get my food to go just so I wouldn't have to sit in the same restaurant with Nora. I can't eat with someone hating me."

Doctor Z didn't say anything in response. She just looked at me in her gentle way.

"I wish I could forget about Nora and how she won't forgive me when I abject begged her to," I went on. "The only time I don't think about it is when I'm with Noel."

"How so?"

I paused, looking for the right words. "When Noel's voice is on the phone," I said, "or his name is in my e-mail, or his hand is holding mine—I feel this full out, flat-on *happiness*. It's like he cancels out all the badness from the past two years at school, like he cancels out all my hateful thoughts and neuroses, like he's my flashlight in a dark city."

25

Doctor Z chewed her Nicorette thoughtfully. "I'm glad he makes you happy," she finally said. "But I do have a concern about your flashlight metaphor."

"How come?"

"Well," she asked, "what happens if your flashlight goes out?"

4

The Revelation About Gay Chinese Penguins!

What to Do with Your Real Live Boyfriend in the Dark: for those moments when you're alone, you want to make out or you don't want to make out, or you've just made out and now you don't know what to say, or the whole making-out thing is going too fast—or not fast enough.

(Instructions given by Meghan, Queen of Real Live Boyfriends, and transcribed by Roo for future use)

1. Just wait. Don't talk. Don't leap out of the car, the room, whatever. Don't start kissing him like a kissing maniac, either, just to fill the time. Be there in the moment. See what happens next.
2. Alternatively, attack him like a kissing maniac. It is a fair bet that he will not think this is a bad idea.
3. Put your hand on his leg. Just leave it there. This will probably make *him* attack you like a kissing maniac.
4. If his hand is going where you don't want it to go, just move it.

This is perfectly good manners in a horizontal situation. If you have to move it more than twice, you can interrupt whatever's going on and say: "Hello. I am moving your hand for a reason, you big dodo," or something of that nature that is flirtatious and firm at the same time.

5. If you're there in the dark together and it's more of a talking situation, don't ask: "What are you thinking?" For some reason, most guys are moronically incapable of answering this simple question. Instead, say something like: "I've always wanted to go to India." Or "I want to bungee jump someday." And see what he says.

   In the dark is a good place to talk about your dreams. Or his.

6. If you are getting to the upper or nether regions, there will be buttons and zippers and suchlike to negotiate. Do not just let him fumble around with your bra clasp or your shirt button for like six hours. He is not enjoying it. He is feeling superawkward that he cannot manage a simple button like a normal person.

   Just undo them yourself, if you want them undone. Trust me, the guy will be seriously relieved.

7. Likewise, you can just ask him to deal with his own buttons—so you don't have to. Really, everyone will be so much happier.

8. If it gets to the nether regions once, *every single time* after that, have protection in your bag. Just in case. Even if you think there's no way it's going to get *that far*. Because it is way better to be all, "Oh, wait, I have something in my bag for just this situation," than to end up pregnant or with some nasty disease. Believe me, your real live boyfriend will not think you are suddenly a famous slut. He will be majorly glad you came prepared and the whole experience will be like a gazillion times nicer if you are not feeling

worried and guilty for being so lame as to be doing what you're doing without protection.

9. And remember: every single time. Every single single time. Have it in your bag.

—dictated by Meghan and written by me into *The Girl Book*, my sporadically updated journal.

In the middle of the summer, before everything went bad with Noel, my grandma Suzette died. She was Dad's mother, and she lived nearby in Bothell. She wasn't that old—seventy-two—but she had this foot surgery a while ago that kept getting infected and somehow her blood got toxic and blah blah blah I don't really understand it, but eventually it killed her.

She was a good grandma to me. Always had peppermints in her bag and bought me monogrammed stationery. She liked to take me shopping at Laura Ashley until I got old enough to put my foot down about *that* business. When I was younger I used to sleep over at her place when my parents went away for the weekend, and we'd rent old movies together and make popcorn in the microwave. It was Grandma Suzette who introduced me to movies like *The Piano* and *Crimes and Misdemeanors.* And before that, to musicals like *My Fair Lady* and comedies like *The Seven Year Itch.*

She loved her DVD player, Grandma Suzette.

Too much, probably. She didn't get out a whole lot, and physically she was something of a mess.

Mom, Dad and I used to drive over there fairly often and take her out to this Italian restaurant where they had unlimited garlic bread. She would take any that was left-over home in a doggy bag.

Anyway, she died of this infection thing. I guess old people do that. Their systems are weak, so they get an infection when a young person wouldn't, and the infection won't heal, and their blood goes toxic or something and then they're just dead.

We visited her in the hospital a few times before it happened, and my throat felt completely closed with tears that weren't coming out because she looked so bony and gray, like her skin was made of crumpled tissue paper. I told her I loved her and brought her a metal box of peppermints and then it was really hard to know what to say–because she was so sick it just seemed wrong to tell her about my day, and we couldn't make plans for the future because although we didn't *know* she was going to die, it seemed pretty likely at that point, and generally it was just agony.

The last thing she said to me was "I'm going to take a nap now. Don't drink my orange juice."

I didn't drink her juice, but we had to go home before she woke up and thirty-six hours later she was dead.

"Don't drink my orange juice."

That was it.

It wasn't a real goodbye.

It was so unfinished.

I hate it when things are unfinished. When you're

not sure what people meant. Why did she think I would drink her orange juice? I had never tried to drink her orange juice.

Or had I? Drunk some once, back when I was a little kid, and she was remembering that time?

●

There was going to be a funeral. My sick alcoholic uncle Hanson came up from Portland. He always makes my dad really tense, he's such a messed-up guy, and he stayed in a hotel but we had to have him over for dinner. He brought his own bottle of whisky and drank the whole thing right in the middle the meal like it was normal. But his mother had just died and it wasn't exactly the time for an intervention, plus Dad has already talked to him about his drinking like a million times and Hanson never listened. All in all it was a pretty shattering weekend.

The funeral was at this place in Bothell near Grandma Suzette's condo, and it was surprising how much Bible stuff was in the speeches people gave, given that we're Christian but we don't go to church. I was wearing a black dress and a dark blue cotton sweater and sitting in the front row with my parents, but I knew Noel and Meghan and our friend Hutch were in the back because I rode with them to the funeral parlor in Meghan's Jeep.

I cried at the funeral because people were giving these speeches where they stood up and talked about Grandma. And her friends stood up, these old ladies, and spoke about how much they had loved her and whatever. It was just really sad.

After it was over we all had to drive to the cemetery and I was in the bathroom trying to get my face to stop shining after the tears, putting powder on my nose, when Meghan called in, "They're making me move my car. Can you get a ride with your parents?"

I said yes, but then when I left the bathroom I couldn't see my parents anywhere. The area in front of the funeral parlor was a sea of people dressed in black, old women with dyed hair putting their hands on each other's arms, cousins of my dad's looking faded and balding, a few little girls running underfoot wearing white tights on chubby legs. I ran outside and looked for our Honda. It was gone.

I didn't want to get into a car with Hanson so I stood up on the porch and surveyed my options. Who else could give me a ride?

There was Nora Van Deusen. Standing by a hedge and not talking to anyone. There with her hands at her sides, staring into space awkwardly.

Nora.

Nora had come to my grandma's funeral.

She saw me just as I saw her, and loped over. Nora is five eleven and has tremendous hooters. She was poured somewhat awkwardly into a navy dress that she probably got for church a year ago. It no longer really fit. She was holding a bouquet of white roses.

"Hi," she said when she got to me.

"Hey." I didn't know what to say.

"I'm really sorry about your grandma," said Nora.

"She was such a kind person." She thrust the flowers into my hands, not meeting my eyes.

Nora knew Grandma Suzette because she and I had been friends from third grade until the end of junior year. You know people's grandmas when you're friends for that long. She'd even had sleepovers at Grandma Suzette's, and the two of us had stayed up late playing with the practically a hundred drugstore lipsticks Grandma had in her bathroom. And freshman year, Grandma took me, Kim, Cricket and Nora to see *The Nutcracker* at Pacific Northwest Ballet, even though we were kind of too old for it by then.

"How did you know she died?" I asked.

"Meghan told me."

"Oh."

"I'm really sorry for your loss," Nora said. Because that's the thing to say at funerals, I guess.

We stood there for a few moments in silence. "How's your summer been?" she finally asked me.

"Pretty good. Aside from the death," I said. "How's yours?"

"Did I tell you I met a guy?"

"You haven't been speaking to me," I reminded her.

Nora blushed. "I met a guy."

Oh.

That's why she wasn't so mad at me anymore.

It wasn't that she missed me so much she decided to forgive me.

She had stopped liking Noel.

"I met him at Sunny Meadows," Nora went on.

Sunny Meadows was a day camp connected to Nora's church. She was a sports leader for them that summer, until August, when her parents would take her to Decatur Island.

"That's great," I said.

"He goes to Lakeside," she said. "His name is–don't laugh."

"What?"

"Say you won't laugh."

"I won't laugh."

"His name is Happy. Happy Mackenzie."

I had heard of Happy Mackenzie, actually. He was stroke for the Lakeside heavy eight, and Jackson, who was a rower, had been at some kind of crew team sports intensive with him. It's not the kind of name people forget.

"And is it a thing thing?" I asked.

"We went out twice last week," Nora said. "And I see him every day at Sunny Meadows. So yeah."

"A thing thing."

"Pretty much so." She grinned.

Nora has never had a boyfriend her whole entire life. Not that she isn't attractive–she's got gorgeous curls and huge boobs and she understands basketball, plus she can bake–but somehow she's never gone out with anyone. "That's really great," I said.

This was like, the most generic thing anyone could say in such a situation, but Nora and I had been angry at each other for so long I didn't feel like I could just dive in and interrogate her about Happy's kissing ability or his giant crew muscles or any of the things I would normally want to know about.

"Did you read about the gay male penguins at the Chinese zoo?" I asked.

Nora looked at me funny. "No."

"Yeah, well, there are gay penguins. That's a documented fact. But these particular gay penguins kept trying to steal eggs from the straight penguins."

Nora looked at me like: where was I going with this?

"They would steal an egg and leave behind a rock as substitute," I continued. "To try and trick the biological parents. Then the gay ones would adopt the egg. Zookeepers kept taking away the egg and giving it back to the bio parents, and they kept stealing another one, again and again."

Nora shook her head in disbelief.

"It's true," I said. "Finally the gay couple had to be segregated from the other penguins with a little picket fence, because they wouldn't stop trying to get a baby of their own."

"Okay. What's the point?"

"The point is, they shouldn't have done what they were doing, and even though they were penguins, they probably knew it; I mean, they were doing the worst, meanest possible thing to their friends and neighbors— but they just couldn't stop, because they wanted a baby so, so desperately."

"What happened?" asked Nora.

"Well, for a while they were ostracized, but finally zookeepers gave them an egg to take care of, from a straight penguin couple that had rejected one. And the gay penguins were so happy! They turned out to be excellent dads."

"Cool." Nora shifted from side to side.

"I mean, penguins in general are excellent dads. The dads hatch the eggs, pretty much. But my point is these guys weren't sociopaths or crazy penguins or anything. They just couldn't behave like normal people when they wanted a baby more than anything in the world. It was like the intense wanting made them psycho."

"Ruby."

"What?"

"You still haven't gotten to the point."

"I'm the gay Chinese penguins," I said. "That's the point."

"What?"

"I know what it's like to want something so desperately you feel like you can't stop trying to get it," I explained, "even when it's not supposed to be yours. I know what it's like to do something wrong, really wrong, because you want the thing so badly you can't help it. And I know what it's like to have everyone hate you for doing it too."

"People can help things," said Nora quietly. "Saying you couldn't help it isn't fair."

Ouch.

"You made a choice to take Noel," she said. "Don't act like it wasn't a choice."

Okay.

Was that true?

Can people help behaving badly? Are we always able to say no?

My uncle Hanson can no longer help himself. Alcohol grips him and makes him do things—like it's bigger than him and he's weak in comparison with it.

But shouldn't he be stronger? Shouldn't he quit, or join a program, or get therapy, or something? Is he, in some way, *choosing* alcoholism the way Nora was saying I chose to pursue Noel?

If you think the person can't help it, you can forgive him more easily.

If you think the person *should* help it, you get angry.

But if you think the person can't help it, they're probably not going to change.

And if you think he *should* help it, there's some hope.

"Maybe it's easier for some people to help things than others," I said to Nora. "I think it's easier for you than for a lot of people."

"Possibly," said Nora. "But I don't think the penguins should have stolen eggs."

Part of me wanted to say: You should have forgiven me ages ago. You should have tried harder to understand me. Noel never liked you back, so he was never yours to start with.

But then I thought: She came to the funeral. And I

am not at all sure that after everything that happened between us, I would have come if it was *Nora's* grandma who died.

For all her rules and accusations, Nora is definitely the kind of person who will show up at a funeral. And say the right thing. And bring flowers.

She had done that today. Which was something like an apology.

So I decided not to ask for another.

"I'm sorry I'm a gay Chinese penguin," I said.

We looked around, and most of the cars had cleared out, driving over to the cemetery. The lawn in front of the funeral parlor was empty.

"Do you have the car?" Nora asked.

"No. My parents ditched me," I said.

"So you need a ride?"

"Uh-huh."

We got into Nora's car, which was a silver Saab—very clean except for a back window cluttered with stickers that read EVERGREEN STATE COLLEGE, TATE PREP B-BALL and other team-spirited-type things. We couldn't see any of the procession that was heading out, but we had directions on a printed sheet of paper from the undertaker, so Nora pulled into traffic.

It was awkward in the car.

We didn't know what to say to each other.

It wasn't clear if we could really be friends or if being on speaking terms was the best we could hope for.

We pulled into the line of cars as it was entering the

cemetery. Moving slowly, we snaked through and eventually stopped near a path that led up to an open grave with a coffin beside it. Grandma's friends began to get out of their cars. All wearing black, they walked gingerly up the steep pathway. A few of them were crying. Others were chitchatting. I looked for Noel, Hutch and Meghan, but I couldn't see them. That was probably for the best, since having Noel and Nora together would have made things even more awkward than they were.

"I need to give my condolences to your parents," said Nora.

"They're probably up at the top already," I said. "We were the last car."

Nora and I trudged up the hill in silence. Some of Grandma's friends moved very slowly, and it didn't seem right to pass them. When we got to the top, we gathered round the grave. It was crowded enough that I couldn't really see, but I half listened to a funeral home guy read a passage from the Bible.

I thought about Grandma Suzette and how she loved me even though she didn't really know what went on in my life. How she didn't know how neurotic I could be, or how bad things had gotten with my friends, or what my sense of humor was really like. She just knew I was Ruby, and my face looked like my dad's, and she loved me 'cause I was her grandchild. My actual personality didn't much matter.

I was crying and Nora was giving me a tissue when

we heard the pastor say: "Alvin Hyman Fudgewick, may you rest in peace."

Wait.

Alvin Hyman Fudgewick?

We were in the wrong place.

In the wrong line of cars, at the wrong grave site, in the right cemetery, at the wrong funeral.

Alvin Hyman Fudgewick's.

"Alvin Hyman Fudgewick is not my grandma," I whispered to Nora. I grabbed her elbow. We walked away as quickly as we possibly could, before bursting into smothered laughter at the bottom of the hill.

"Quiet!" whispered Nora. "Alvin Hyman Fudgewick is dead and he would not like us laughing at his funeral."

I snorted. "We are horrible people. I can't believe we're laughing."

"Where is your family?"

"I have no idea."

"Should we look for them?"

"Probably. Shall we tell them about Alvin?"

"You can't call him Alvin," said Nora. "You don't even know him. You have to call him Mr. Fudgewick."

"I cried at his funeral. I think I can call him Alvin."

Nora paused. Then she just said: "Alvin Hyman Fudgewick."

I burst out laughing.

We got back into Nora's car and drove around the cemetery. Whenever it seemed too quiet, or there was a pause in the conversation, one of us would say "Alvin Hyman Fudgewick" and we'd collapse into giggles.

It was me and Nora.

Not the way we had been. We might not ever be like that again.

But laughing, which is something we'd always been good at together.

Alvin Hyman Fudgewick.

Alvin Hyman Fudgewick.

Eventually, we found my family, far at the other end of the graveyard.

My dad was sobbing on Hutch's shoulder.

Grandma Suzette was already in the ground.

Uncle Hanson was drinking from a flask, sitting on the hood of his rental car.

My mom was furious with me.

I didn't feel like laughing anymore.

●

Another video clip:

Hutch is in Kevin Oliver's greenhouse repotting a bonsai tree. His haircut is growing out and he has it tied off his face with a blue bandana. His acne flares in the summer heat, so his forehead and chin look swollen and irritated.

> *Roo: (behind the camera) I'm asking people to define words for me. It's a project for my film school applications. You're my first victim.*
> *Hutch: Rock on.*

Roo: So. What's your definition of love?

Hutch: (laughs) Nature's way of tricking people into
reproducing.

Roo: Come on.

Hutch: A reason people kill themselves.

Roo: Ahem. Would you like to know why you're single?

Hutch: (smiles regretfully) Oh, I know why I'm single.

Hutch has been going to school with me since kindergarten. He's been a roly-poly[1] since seventh grade due to a tragic case of acne, the cruelty of middle schoolers and a tendency to quote retro metal lyrics in place of making ordinary human conversation. He works for my dad as an assistant gardener, and somehow we've become friends.

Just from proximity, I guess.

And because everyone else at Tate Prep shuns us.

Anyway, Hutch is funny, once he starts talking. He doesn't like his parents much, and they don't seem to like him either, since they never come to any school events. He seems to think hanging out with my dad and eating raw food for dinner at our house is preferable to whatever he might be doing at home, so he's around a fair amount. I'm taking his cinematic education in hand. We made our own documentary film festival that we named The Kirk Hammett Festival of Truth and Glory,

---

[1] Roly-poly: A roly-poly is a bug, technically a woodlouse, that curls up in a hard little ball if you touch it. But what I mean is, Hutch is a social outcast.

Hammett being Hutch's favorite guitar player and subject of the best movie in our whole series: *Metallica: Some Kind of Monster,* which is all about a dysfunctional metal band in group psychotherapy. We also saw this film about a guy who lived with grizzly bears (until they ate him) and another about all the incredible grossness of fast food.[2]

More from the Hutch interview in the greenhouse:

Roo: What's your definition of popularity?

Hutch: I used to think people were popular because they were good-looking, or nice, or funny, or good at sports.

Roo: Aren't they?

Hutch: I'd think, If I could just be those things, I'd—you know—have more friends than I do. But in seventh grade, when Jackson and those guys stopped hanging out with me, I tried as hard as I could to get them to like me again. But then . . . (shaking his head as if to clear it) I don't really wanna talk about it.

Roo: What happened?

Hutch: They just did some ugly stuff to me is all. And really, it was for the best.

Roo: Why?

Hutch: Because I was cured. I realized the popular people weren't nice or funny or great-looking. They just had power, and they actually got the power by teasing

42

---

[2] In case you care: *Grizzly Man* and *Super Size Me.* We watched a bunch of others, too, but those were the best.

people or humiliating them—so people bonded to them
out of fear.

Roo: Oh.

Hutch: I didn't want to be a person who could act like
that. I didn't want to ever speak to any person who
could act like that.

Roo: Oh.

Hutch: So then I wasn't trying to be popular anymore.

Roo: Weren't you lonely?

Hutch: I didn't say it was fun. (He bites his thumbnail,
bonsai dirt and all.) I said it was for the best.

After Grandma's funeral, and after Hanson went home to crawl into whatever hole he lives in, Dad had to clear through Grandma's things and field condolence notes from all her friends. One afternoon, he came home from walking Polka-dot with tears streaming down his face.

The next day I found him weeping into a pot of miniature roses. And from then on it was pretty typical to have him sobbing into his salad at dinner, or to find him lying on the couch in the morning, insomniac, staring at the ceiling fan with a quivering lip.

Mom got progressively impatient with him—she'd say things like "Kevin, if you have to sob, do it in the bedroom. I'm trying to write an e-mail here" and "Kevin, blow your nose like an adult human being, won't you? There's no reason there should be snotty tissues on the table while I'm trying to eat my kiwi."

"He was always overly attached to her," Mom said one day when she was driving me to my job at the Woodland Park Zoo. Polka was sticking his ginormous head out the back window of the Honda.

"She was his *mother*," I said. "She *died*."

"Yeah," said Mom. "But Kevin has always been something of a mama's boy. That's why he's such a wreck now that she's gone. Overattachment."

"Shouldn't people be attached?" I asked. "Isn't that the point of human relationships, to be attached?"

"Well, there's such a thing as too much," she said, pulling off the freeway. "Still"—she checked her eye makeup in the rearview mirror—"he'll get better in a couple days, I bet. Don't worry."

"I'm not worried."

"Yes, you are."

"No, I'm not."

But I was.

And Dad didn't get better in a couple of days. He got a lot worse.

5

Agony and Love Poems!

a video clip:

Noel sits before an outdoor table at the coffee shop down the road from Roo's house. In front of him is a sesame bagel with cheddar cheese. His favorite.

> *Noel: Whenever you're ready.*
> *Roo: (behind the camera) So. How do you define . . .*
>   *friendship?*
> *Noel: (bitterly) My dad says it's something that gets in the*
>   *way of a business deal.*
> *Roo: Ag.*
> *Noel: Yeah. Well. That's probably why he's divorced.*
> *Roo: No kidding.*
> *Noel: And my brother Claude says friendship is a method*
>   *of castration that doesn't use a sharp object.*

Roo: Huh?

Noel: Like, friendship is a word girls use when they want to turn down guys. As in, "Oh, I can't go out with you because I'm afraid of what it will do to our friendship."

Roo: Oh.

Noel: Or in Claude's case, guys use it to turn down guys.

Roo: But how do you define it?

Noel: A lot of people see friends as something you have on Twitter or Facebook or wherever. If someone wants to read your updates and you want to read their updates, then you're friends. You don't ever have to see each other. But that seems like a stupid definition to me.

Roo: Yeah.

Noel: Although on the other hand, rethink. Maybe a friend is someone who wants your updates. Even if they're boring. Or sad. Or annoyingly cutesy. A friend says "Sign me up for your boring crap, yes indeed"— because he likes you anyway. He'll tolerate your junk.

Roo: You have a lot of friends.

Noel: No, I don't.

Roo: You do. You know everyone at school. You get invited to parties.

Noel: I get invited to parties, yeah. And I know people. But I don't want their updates.

Roo: Oh.

Noel: And I sincerely doubt they want mine.

Roo: I want your updates.

Noel: I want your updates. (He looks down, bashfully.) I do. I want all your updates, Ruby.

Roo: Trust me. You don't want them all.

Noel: I do. Even the boring ones.

Roo: It's not the boring ones that are the problem. It's the crazy ones.

Noel: (shakes his head disbelievingly)

Roo: I have some very deeply mental updates, Noel. You don't need to be around for those.

Noel: You're not mental. You think you're mental. That's a different thing.

Roo: Isn't that mental?

Noel: Can I have the updates, please? I said I wanted all the updates.

Roo: (laughing) Fine. Your funeral.

Noel was leaving Seattle for most of August. He was headed to New York City to stay with his brother Claude and Claude's boyfriend Booth on the Lower East Side. He had gone last year and the year before, too. He and Claude were really close.

Noel talked about his brother like he was golden. Smart and brave. Comfortable in school or in nightclubs or biking the dangerous streets of New York City. A sharp dresser. I think Claude treated Noel like a grown-up, even though they were almost four years apart. Made him feel like his opinion mattered.

Booth and Claude were a funny couple, Noel said. Booth was bitter and probably partied more than was good for anybody, while Claude was quieter: idealistic, a dreamer. Still, they had been each other's real live boyfriend since the end of their freshman year of college. Now they were juniors and had a four-bedroom apartment with a bunch of fellow students in a converted factory, living in what Noel described as "domestic bliss and squalor."

Noel was *my* real live boyfriend, so when he got to New York he called me on his cell from places like the Guggenheim, a cheap dumpling place in Chinatown, a flea market in Chelsea—leaving messages on our machine saying he was thinking of me.[1] His e-mails were full of rhymes he made up, links to silliness on the Internet, descriptions of the city.

Number of languages heard on the street yesterday: 8. English, Spanish, Portuguese (I think), Russian, French, German, Japanese, Chinese.

Number of miles Booth and I biked yesterday, going to the Met and home again: probably 10.

Number of pizza slices consumed while walking, since arrival: 6.

Minutes spent staring at the water lily painting in the MoMA: 13.

---

[1] I missed his calls because I am the last person on the planet without a cell phone. My parents insist that if I want one I have to pay for it. But I got the video camera instead.

Number of Spider-Man-shaped ice creams bought from the truck on the corner of Broadway and Prince: 1.

Number of guys actually dressed as Spider-Man I saw *while eating the ice cream*: 1.

(I love New York.)

(But I miss you.)

Noel

Then one day, a day like any other as far as I knew, he didn't pick up when I called his cell.

Later that day, he still hadn't replied to my last two e-mails.

Next day, he didn't answer his cell or call me back.

And the day after that, still nothing.

The day after that was my seventeenth birthday, and I was sure Noel would call, or a present would arrive, or something. My parents gave me a stack of mystery novels and a new Speedo for swim team, but because of Mom's raw food obsession, there wasn't any cake. There were dehydrated banana-barley cookies with candles.

I couldn't even laugh at them.

Hutch drove over in the evening and brought me a cupcake.

I cried because it wasn't from Noel.

Why hadn't he called?

He knew when my birthday was.

It was so strange, his sudden absence from my life.

The day after my birthday, a short e-mail made everything wonderful again, if only for a moment:

I miss you
like a limb
like a leg I've lost
in a war, maybe
in an accident, maybe
in a tragedy.
But I can still feel my leg,
pumping with blood,
itching to move.
I can still feel it,
so that I think it is there,
still part of my body,
and when I wake up in the morning
I am surprised to remember it's gone.
Then I am sad,
and disabled without it.
I limp through my day,
off balance,
needing it.

He'd sent me a love poem.

A weird and bloody love poem, but a love poem.

I tried to write him back a poem, but I couldn't. I didn't feel inspired, the way Noel must have: biking the streets of New York, seeing amazing paintings, going to the theater, eating hot pretzels on the street. So I wrote back, but I just wrote about regular stuff. I told him about my birthday presents, and joked about the foul barley cookies, and told about Hutch and the cupcake.

Actually: I'm not telling you the whole truth.

I was still mad he hadn't called me back, I guess. And hadn't answered my e-mails. I'd spent the last few days wondering if he'd call, wondering why he *didn't* call.

So I was angry.

Even though I loved the poem.

Even though it had made me happy for a few minutes.

What I wrote back was meant to make him feel guilty. For my lonely birthday. The sadness of no cake. The fact that Hutch had shown up and done what Noel should have done. I wrote it all as if I were cheerful as could be—just "Let me tell you this funny story about yesterday"—but all the cheer was fake. Secretly, I wanted him to read the e-mail and notice he'd forgotten my birthday and feel horrible and make it up to me.

Later, I would wonder, over and over, what would have happened if I'd written Noel a poem back.

Or even an honestly angry note.

If, instead of being fake and cheerful to cover up how hurt I was, I had been raw and true and told him everything that was in my heart.

Anyway, he didn't write back.

For one day. Two. Three.

I called.
He still wasn't picking up his phone.
Then one day, another e-mail:

Sixteen days (I've been gone)
Plus eight more days (till I come back).
That's twenty-four days,
A ridiculous number of hours,
an insane number of minutes,
when every minute lasts an hour
and every hour lasts a day.
The clocks have nearly stopped themselves.
No batteries will speed them up.
No power boost, no winding.
They hardly move, these clocks.
Watching the hands go round is like
watching someone's blood drip onto the street
while you wait for an ambulance
and wait
and wait
and the blessed siren does not sound.
The clocks will hardly move
and hardly move
and hardly move
Until
I
am
home.
Maybe when I see you they will start again.

Oh.

Wow.

That.

For me.

How can you be mad at a guy who writes you a poem like that?

Most people would say you can't. Noel was so honest on the page. When I first read his words, I felt like he was reaching out to me through them.

Except, when I thought about it later—he wasn't. Not really.

1. He loves me! Poemy poem goodness! Romance!
2. No. If he loved you, he'd call you back.
3. Maybe his phone broke.
4. Then he'd e-mail you that his phone broke.
5. But a poem! *Two* poems! Romantic poems!
6. Yeah, but what's stopping him from writing you back about Hutch's going-away party? He needs to write back about that. A real live boyfriend would write back about that.
7. Yeah. That's true.
8. He's not writing about *you,* anyway. He's writing about phantom limbs and clocks. The poems could be about anyone.
9. In a way, it's like he's writing to an *idea* of some ideal Ruby who's not really the same as the Ruby who exists.
10. Yeah. Because the Idea of the Ideal Ruby loves the

poems and feels fulfilled, but the Ruby Who Exists really wants to talk to him about Hutch's party.

11. Shouldn't the Ruby Who Exists not be so demanding and just be thankful for the poems?
12. But when he doesn't call me back I feel insecure!
13. He wrote you poems!
14. But he hasn't called.
15. But he wrote you poems!
16. But he hasn't called.

And so on. I was driving myself even more insane than on an ordinary day.

Finally, I just planned the party for Hutch without any input from Noel, and tried to go about my life ignoring the shaky, needy feeling in the center of my chest. I only allowed myself to call Noel's cell once a day.

He never picked up.

At some point I stopped leaving messages.

6.

Distraction Caused by a Bare Chest!

a video clip:

Finn Murphy—barista, soccer stud-muffin, Meghan's boyfriend—stands behind the counter at the B&O Espresso, wearing an apron over a white shirt with the sleeves rolled up. His light blond hair has grown out a bit from his crew cut, and he smiles shyly.

Roo: (behind the camera) You ready?

Finn: Unless a customer comes in.

Roo: I'll be quick. So, what's your definition of love?

Finn: Oh. Ah. Love is trust, I think.

Roo: How so?

Finn: Love is when you give someone else the power to destroy you, and you trust them not to do it.

Roo: Ag.

Finn: Why do you say ag?

Roo: What if they do *destroy you?*

Finn: You have to trust that they won't.

Roo: But what if they do? Was it love, then?

Finn: I don't know. I guess if you trusted them not to, then what you *felt was love, yeah.*

Roo: But what if they didn't destroy you for a while, and then all of a sudden they did destroy you? Was it love for them, before they suddenly went all destructive?

Finn: (laughing) What?

Roo: What about the other person? If they start destroying you, does that mean they never loved you?

Finn: Ah. Maybe?

Roo: Or could they be destroying you by accident, because they love you but don't understand you?

Finn: Ruby–

Roo: Or do you measure love by how they felt in the trust department? Like, they could totally destroy you, but they still loved you because they trusted you *not to destroy* them, *and that's what love is.*

Finn: Can this be over now?

Roo: Are you sure we should be giving anyone the power to destroy *us?*

Finn: Ruby.

Roo: What?

Finn: Can this please *be over?*

Roo: Why?

One day, while all that badness was happening with
Noel not answering his phone, Gideon Van Deusen
showed up shirtless on the dock of our houseboat. I was
helping in the greenhouse, because Meghan was off
with Finn as usual and Dad was seriously behind in
photographing his summer blooms for the newsletter.
Instead of working, he was moping around all day saying stuff like: "My mother always kept her kitchen sink
clean." And "My mother will never get to see this year's
gardenias."

I was trying to make a short video for his blog
(*Container Gardening for the Rare Bloom Lover* had finally
gone digital) that would rotate 360 degrees through his
greenhouse, enabling all six of his maniacally loyal fans to
have the full-surround experience of the "plant haven" he
has been writing about. Hutch was hiding the junky old
CD player and various other unsightly things that would
mar the beauty of the shot, and I had just stepped out to
film the exterior when I heard a speedboat putt-putt up to
the dock.

Gideon hopped out wearing nothing but a pair of
board shorts and a bead choker. His dark brown hair
was wet and hung over his face. I had never seen him
without a shirt on and for a second I didn't recognize
him. Maybe it was the wet hair and maybe it was the

bead choker of my seventh-grade fantasies. Or maybe it was just his extremely nice-looking bare chest. In any case, I thought: It's Tommy Hazard.

The surfer-boy version of Tommy Hazard, all grown up.

I must be hallucinating.

But then he said, "Ruby, hey. How are ya? We're nearly out of gas. Isn't there a station up at the top of the hill?"—and I realized it was Nora's brother.

"Hi, Gideon," I said. Meaning: Nice abs. "Yeah, there's a station. Do you have a can to put the gas in?"

I looked at the boat, where two more shirtless guys were tying up to the dock. They headed toward us, one dark-skinned and slightly heavy with long dreaded hair, one Caucasian and beaky, carrying a presumably empty gas can; both were clearly friends of Gideon's from Evergreen. I could tell by their sideburns, hemp bracelets and sandaled feet.

"Yeah, we got a can," said Gideon. "We were wakeboarding in the middle of the lake when I suddenly realized we're on empty. It didn't seem safe to try to make it all the way across to fill her up. We might have gotten stranded. So we docked here."

The two guys waved at me as they headed up the hill carrying the gas can, while Gideon shook the water out of his hair and smiled down at me. Very Tommy Hazard. "What are you filming?"

"I'm making a video for my dad's gardening Web site," I said. "How come you're not going with them?" I tipped my head to where his friends were pushing through the gate that led to the street.

Gideon laughed. "I didn't bring any shoes."

"Well. It gets you out of having to hike up the hill to the station."

"True. Hey, do you have a Band-Aid I can borrow?"

Now this is going to sound insane, but a part of me was surprised that Gideon Van Deusen, who traveled the world for a year before starting college, who questioned the teachings of his Sunday school back in ninth grade, who played guitar badly and didn't mind being bad at it, who folded his laundry so neatly, who had been class speaker at Tate Prep the year he graduated and who obviously spent quite a serious amount of time doing sit-ups—I was surprised that Gideon Van Deusen, who seemed so well-balanced and comfortable in himself—would need a Band-Aid.

He seemed so perfect to me, I guess. An older guy who's got it together. A guy so confident in himself that it seems impossible he'd have a hole in his skin. A hole that might actually be bleeding.

"You can't borrow one," I told him. "But you can have one to keep."

He laughed and I showed him into the houseboat. Polka remembered him from the one time he'd been over to visit and slurped Gideon's hands.

I went to the bathroom to get Band-Aids, but before I went back to the living room, I stopped and put on lip gloss. I thought:

1. What? I have no lip gloss on. My lips feel dry. This lip gloss has nothing to do with Gideon.
2. Oh, fine. There is a shirtless college boy bleeding in my living room. I want lip gloss.
3. I can still be in love with Noel and want a shirtless college boy to think I am good-looking, can't I?
4. Or maybe I can't.
5. Maybe if you're really in love, you don't care if anyone thinks you're good-looking besides the person you're in love *with*.
6. Maybe it's deranged to want college boys to think you're hot when you already have a boyfriend.
7. Maybe I am a sex maniac slut like everybody says.
8. And then again, it's just lip gloss.

I brought out a box of Band-Aids with pictures of sushi on them, along with some antibiotic ointment. Gideon showed me a spot on his calf where the wakeboard had flipped and sliced him. It wasn't big, but it would need two Band-Aids to cover it.

"Are you a sushi fan?" Gideon asked.

"No," I said truthfully. "I just like silly Band-Aids. I got these at Archie McPhee. They have pirate ones and bacon ones, too."

I squeezed some ointment on my finger.

Gideon looked surprised. "You don't have to do that," he said.

"Oh," I said, embarrassed. "You're probably capable of putting a Band-Aid on yourself, aren't you?

"I *am* experienced in that department."

"It's an impulse left over from babysitting."

"Okay, go ahead." He stuck out his leg. "So. You babysit?"

"Not anymore. I couldn't take it. The kid I used to sit for was like a blood and vomit machine."

Gideon laughed. "A patent on that idea could make a fortune."

"Yeah," I said. "Or his parents could just rent him out. Like whenever anyone needs blood or vomit, they could just come over and rent out Kai."

All this while I was dabbing ointment on Gideon's calf, which was tan and covered in light brown hair. I thought:

1. His skin is surprisingly soft.
2. But also hairy.
3. Gideon is practically an adult. I think he's at least nineteen.
4. Is it horrible that I want to touch his leg?
5. I mean, Doctor Z says it's completely normal at my age to have this level of Rabbit Fever, but what I really want to know is, am I being disloyal?
6. It is only ointment, after all.
7. And a Band-Aid.
8. Then again, I wouldn't like it if Noel was spreading ointment on the bare calves of Ariel Olivieri.
9. Especially not if Ariel was wearing nothing but a bathing suit and a bead choker.

I was just putting a second Band-Aid on Gideon's leg, and enjoying it more than I should have, when

61

Hutch walked in from the greenhouse. I jerked back guiltily.

"Gideon Van Deusen," Hutch announced, barely making eye contact while he went to the sink and filled his water bottle. "Rock on."

Gideon looked blank. "Have we met?" he asked Hutch.

"This is John Hutchinson," I said apologetically.

Hutch hopped up on the counter and swigged his water, still without making eye contact.

Gideon held out his hand. "Good to meet you."

"We've met," said Hutch, shaking it.

"I have a bad memory for faces."

"We went to school together for ten years."

"Oh, yeah," said Gideon, obviously lying. "Out of context. Sorry."

This is why Hutch is such a roly-poly. He has zero sense of what a warped little bunny he sounds like sometimes.

Yes, they had been at school together. But Gideon had graduated when we were freshmen, and seniors can't be expected to recall every dorkface underclassman from three years ago. But there went Hutch, saying Gideon's whole name like a semi-stalker, and then telling him to "Rock on," not even saying hello like a normal person. And then what kind of conversationalist quick-calculates the number of years their Tate Prep careers overlapped and uses it to guilt the other person for not remembering?

"Did you finish getting the greenhouse set up?" I asked Hutch, to change the subject. "And is Dad presentable?"

"His face is dry, at least. And yeah. It looks pretty good in there."

"Gideon's boat ran out of gas," I explained.

"Almost," said Gideon.

We all stood around the kitchen for a moment. Not saying anything. Then Hutch said, "Nice lip gloss, Ruby," jumped off the counter and went back outside.

What?

Why was he commenting on my lip gloss?

Since when did Hutch notice my lips anyway?

"Was that your boyfriend?" asked Gideon, plopping himself on our couch and stroking Polka's ears.

"No," I said, sitting down on the rocking chair. "Why?"

"He seemed a little tense is all."

"He's—he's a friend of my boyfriend's," I explained. "He's just being protective."

Realizing: Oh. That's what "Nice lip gloss" meant.

It meant, "Ruby, you're going out with Noel, remember?"

"So you have a boyfriend?" Gideon asked. He leaned forward and touched the hem of my sundress with the tips of his fingers.

"I—I think I do," I answered.

I have a boyfriend who doesn't call me back, I thought.

I have a boyfriend who doesn't answer my e-mails.

"You think, or you know?" asked Gideon, looking up at me.

"I don't exactly know right now," I said. "The thing—it's hard to explain. The thing we have is somehow not the thing it was before."

At that juncture, a shout of "Gas!" could be heard from the deck. The guys had come back and were going to refill the boat.

"You should call me," Gideon said, standing up to leave. "When you know for sure."

"For sure, what?"

"For sure you don't have a boyfriend."

"What if I do?" I asked. "I mean, I am pretty sure I do."

"Then don't call me." He was standing in our doorway, silhouetted in the light. "But call me."

7

Humiliation at Snappy Dragon!

a video clip:

Meghan sits in the window seat of her bedroom. The Tiffany blue wall behind her is decorated with photographs and mementos. Her silky curls are up on top of her head and she's wearing one of Finn's soccer T-shirts.

> *Ruby: (behind the camera) What's your definition of love?*
> *Meghan: I didn't know you were going to ask hard questions.*
> *Roo: This is a serious documentary.*
> *Meghan: (twisting her hair with her fingers) Okay. Love is . . . Um. Love is this feeling. It's a big feeling. It's like listening to music, you know, like a ballad or*

even religious music—because it fills you up and you
can't think about anything but the other person and
it all seems like a dream. Finn took me out in a
canoe the other day, and we had a picnic and
watched the sunset. That's like love in action.

Roo: Isn't that love in the movies?

Meghan: What do you mean?

Roo: Isn't real love something different?

Meghan: I don't think so. I think the movies are
expressing the way love feels, the beauty of it.

Roo: Sunsets and picnics. Really?

Meghan: Don't be cynical. I've been in love twice. I think
I know how it feels.

Roo: It doesn't feel that way to me.

Meghan: Doesn't it?

Roo: No.

Meghan: Are you sure it's love, then?

Hutch was going away. He was spending the first half of senior year on an exchange program in Paris, and I got the idea to have a goodbye party, partly to cheer up my dad and partly to be nice to Hutch. There weren't many people to invite—just me, Noel, Meghan and my parents—but I thought it was a fine excuse for cake, and we could get him travel-type presents, like a French guidebook or a fanny pack.

Hutch in a fanny pack would be very amusing.

Anyway, he was leaving in late August, the day after Noel was supposed to come back from New York, so the party had to happen the night of Noel's return. I decided we'd all go to Judy Fu's Snappy Dragon, our favorite Chinese place, and then to Simply Desserts, where they have the most unbelievable white chocolate cake. I invited Hutch and Meghan, told my parents and sent Noel this e-mail:

> 7 pm, day you get back
> Judy Fu's, a goodbye thing for Hutch.
> We can pick you up in the Honda if you need.
> Let me know if you can make it.
> Love,
> Roo

Doctor Z is always saying: Think what you want out of a situation, and then try to get it. And I wanted Noel to come out with us the moment he got back.

I wanted to sit next to him at Snappy Dragon and twine my leg around his under the table.

I wanted to give him a ride so I'd get to drive him home after dinner, alone.

I wanted to kiss him in the car outside his house for so long my lips felt swollen, drinking him in after so many weeks apart.

So the e-mail was meant to get me all those things, but I was trying to be subtle about it.

And later, I would wonder over and over what would have happened if I hadn't tried to be subtle. If I had been bold and true. If I'd conquered the weirdness

I felt because he hadn't called, and just said: I want to see you more than anything in the world. I'll die if you don't come see me Sunday night. Come be with me, come be with me, come be with me. Noel.

But I didn't. Say that.

And after I sent my subtle e-mail, I thought: He won't come.

I can't assume he wants to come.

No, no. Stop thinking that.

He does want to come.

He will *want* to come.

He's my real live boyfriend.

But he didn't reply.

●

The night of Noel's return, Hutch, Meghan and I drove to Snappy Dragon in Meghan's Jeep, leaving my parents to take the Honda.

"Are we supposed to pick up Noel?" Meghan asked, pushing a CD into the car stereo and pulling out of Hutch's driveway.

I was sitting in the back and I could see Hutch wince in profile as Beyoncé came through the speakers. Hutch and Meghan are friends only of the school variety. They don't hang out unless I'm there to be the link, and Meghan spends a lot of time with Finn and his soccer buddies—a social group in which Hutch would be woefully out of place.

Hutch shrugged. "Haven't talked to him."

"I haven't either," I said. Meghan knew this

already. She asked because she was hoping Hutch would have.

Hutch turned and looked at me, some hurt in his eyes. "I thought you said he was coming."

"I said he *probably* was. I completely invited him."

"Let's call. Do you have his number?"

But Meghan had already found it in her cell.

"DuBoise, are you home?" she asked when Noel answered.

"Don't talk and drive," said Hutch. "Give it to me."

But she didn't hand it over. "It's Meghan, you doof," she said to Noel. "I'm in the car with Roo and Hutch. Do you need a ride?"

Hutch grabbed the phone. "Dude. Welcome back. How was New York?"

I leaned back in my seat and stared out the window, blinking away tears.

Noel was here.

He was here in Seattle and he'd picked up his phone for Meghan when he hadn't picked up for me.

"I'm leaving tomorrow, dude," Hutch was saying. "No more Tate till December."

Silence. Hutch listening.

"Nah, not even Thanksgiving. I thought Ruby explained it all."

Silence again.

"Well, you should check your e-mail. We're going to Snappy Dragon and then some dessert place with white chocolate cake."

Pause.

"I don't like white chocolate either, but Ruby says trust her."

Hutch shook his head as Noel was talking. Then he turned and rolled his eyes at me.

"Whatever, dude. I'll be back in four months. Nah, it's fine."

He hung up.

"Lame!" Meghan said.

"He's jet-lagged," said Hutch. "And he forgot about it. And his parents want him home. He said to tell you he's sorry, Ruby."

He wasn't coming.

He was back in Seattle and he hadn't called and he wasn't coming.

I mean, I kind of knew he wasn't.

But until then, I had been able to hope he was.

I'm a vegetarian, so I ate asparagus in black bean sauce and vegetable pot stickers. Hutch, Meghan and Dad shared mu shu pork and sliced cod in Szechuan sauce, and my mother abandoned her raw food diet because she likes the Snappy smoked duck so much.

It wasn't a very good celebration. Everything tasted like straw because of the choking feeling at the back of my throat. I was trying not to sob and my father was staring morosely into his plate of rice, occasionally saying things like: "My mother used to make asparagus on holidays."

"My mother liked orzo better than rice."

"My mother went to China once."

"My mother used to bleach our tablecloth in the sink."

Mom kept trying to get Dad to change the subject and tell Hutch about how they'd backpacked through Europe before Dad insisted on settling down and building his dream houseboat. "We slept on the trains, John," she told Hutch as he unwrapped a Lonely Planet guide to Paris. "We'd shove our wallets down our shirts so no one could steal them. I didn't shower for days. It was wonderful."

Hutch smiled at her in the way teenagers smile at their friends' parents. "I'm staying with a host family, actually. I'm registered for school there."

"Now I shower almost every day," said my mother. "But it's really not necessary. In Europe it's totally normal to bathe only once a week."

"Don't bathe once a week, Mom," I said.

"Why shouldn't I?" she said. "I wouldn't smell. We just worry about smelling, but really we don't smell."

"What about the smelly people?" I said. "There are definitely people who are smelly."

"You might get a rash," said Meghan. "Like a sweat rash."

"No, I won't," said Mom, taking a sip of tea. "I think it'll be very good for my skin, actually. I have a few dry patches that I'm sure are from overbathing."

"Please, don't let your new thing be refusing to bathe," I said. "Any new thing but that."

"What do you mean my 'new thing'?" my mother snapped.

I knew I was starting an argument.

I knew I was, and I knew I shouldn't.

But I was so shattered about Noel not coming, all the badness had to come out one way or another.

"You know. First it was juice fasting, then craniosacral therapy, then Rolfing, then the macrobiotic diet, then raw food. And now that you're eating *smoked duck,* you'll obviously need some new *thing* to fill the void left when you abandon the raw food way of life."

"Ruby!" My mother straightened up in anger just as Meghan kicked me under the table.

But I kept talking. "So I'm just asking you not to take up no bathing as your thing. I think that's reasonable. It's not a pathway to health and it's not chic and European and it's not anything except gross. You can put lotion on your dry patches and pick a different new thing, no loss."

"I can't believe you're saying this to me."

"Why not? Dad and I have suffered enough through all your fads. I don't think we should have to live with someone who doesn't bathe."

"You!" My mother stood up so quickly her chair fell over and hit the floor with a bang. She shoved her pointer finger in my face and leaned down so her angry mouth was in front of my eyes. "You are a disrespectful, unsympathetic, shallow brat who has no idea what it's like to be searching for something. Searching for some kind of *truth,* some kind of *path* to be on in this life. All you care about is whether you get dessert and whether you can borrow the car and whether some boy is going to call you."

"I want truth," I said, because her words stung. "I want a path. I just don't want to talk to *you* about them."

"What? Why not?"

"You're a crap listener."

"I am a wonderful listener! Ask anyone. Ask Dad. Ask Juana."

"You're not!" I cried. "You're such a bad listener you have to pay Doctor Z to listen to me instead. How many parents have to do that?"

Meghan kicked me under the table again, hard this time.

"I am working extra hours copyediting to pay for that doctor," said my mother. "Do *not* give me attitude about that." She picked up a piece of tea-smoked duck with her fingers and shoved it into her mouth, talking while she chewed. "And do not give me attitude about my choices, either. I want to eat smoked duck now? I eat smoked duck. It is not any of your business to be commenting or criticizing what I choose to eat or how I choose to live."

"I live *with* you!" I cried. "I have eaten raw food for breakfast and dinner every day for months and months. How am I not going to react to that?"

"You're supposed to show respect for what I'm doing," Mom said.

At this juncture in a classic Ruby/Elaine argument, Dad would typically be intervening and saying that yes, it was healthy for us to be sharing our deep feelings, but he thought that maybe we could benefit from some mediation and could he just hear each person's point of view voiced calmly? Only he didn't.

"You don't mean respect," I told her. "You mean you want me to be quiet and let you boss me around the way you boss Dad."

"I do *not* boss your father," said my mother, teeth gritted.

"I'm allowed to say if I want dessert! I can to ask to borrow the car! That's just basic conversation when you live with someone."

"Take it back!"

"What?"

"About your father. Take it back."

"Take it back? We're not in fourth grade here."

"Take it back, Ruby. I do not boss him."

"I'm not taking anything back," I said.

I knew I was being mean.

I knew I had picked a fight and done it in a completely public place, which was horrible.

And I knew I must seem shallow to my mother.

But still, I felt right. She *was* a crap listener. A boss. A follower of fads. She *was all those things*–and just then, at least, it seemed desperately important that someone point that out to her.

"I don't need to take anything back," I said. "Because everything I've said is true."

"Kevin, get the car," my mom said, grabbing his arm and practically yanking him up from the table.

Dad fumbled for his wallet as if wondering how much the meal would cost.

"Don't give her money!" barked Mom. "I can't believe you'd stop to give her money after the way she's acted."

She snatched the wallet from him and marched out of Snappy Dragon. My dad shrugged on his jacket and followed her, mumbling an apology to Hutch.

I stood at our table, choking with rage and embarrassment and wondering how on earth I was going to pay for what must be a seventy-dollar meal with the twenty dollars in my bag.

Then I realized that the figure dressed in black, standing by the cash register, was Noel.

Meghan spotted him when I did and in typical fashion ran up and threw her arms around him in a full-body hug.[1] She grabbed Noel by the arm and pulled him

---

[1] This is precisely the kind of behavior that makes girls generally hate Meghan. Like: Why does she need to be rubbing her sexy body up against my boyfriend's torso? Why?

But I have learned to ignore this aspect of her because she is so freaking nice to me—and in this case, I was grateful. There I was, red-faced with embarrassment, anger and tears, and she was able to act like nothing tragic had happened.

toward our table. He looked wan and tired from the cross-country flight, and he hadn't put any gel in his hair, so it hung down softly over his forehead. He wore a shabby black trench coat I hadn't seen before and a T-shirt that read EASILY DISTRACTED BY SHINY OBJECTS.

"Ruby's mom just had a ginormous fit and yelled at her," Meghan was saying. "I don't know if you saw."

Noel nodded. "I've been here awhile, actually."

Ag.

He saw me say all those horrible things to my mother.

He saw me make a scene in a restaurant.

He saw me ruin Hutch's going-away party.

Ag.

A month ago it would have been fine.

A month ago, Noel was my real live boyfriend and I would have trusted him to understand why I had acted the way I did. Or to forgive me if he didn't understand it.

But now—I was disgusted with myself; there was no reason he wouldn't be disgusted with me. Yet at the same time I felt like screaming at him: It's your fault. Don't you see that? If you'd just called me like a real boyfriend, and showed up here to say goodbye to Hutch like a real friend, I would never have been so lonely inside and tangled. If you had showed up, I never would have yelled at my mother and everything would be fine right now.

But I'm not so crazy that I said that out loud.

"Hi, Ruby," Noel said as I sat there at the food-covered table, staring at him with my eyes overflowing. "It's great to see you."

I couldn't talk.

He was still standing on the other side of the table.

Wasn't he coming around? Wasn't he going to explain, or kiss me so I'd know everything was okay?

Didn't he see I was crying? Wouldn't he take me in his arms?

No, I realized.

He wasn't going to hug me, or kiss me, or even smile at me.

He was just saying "It's great to see you" like a pod-robot. A very, very attractive pod-robot, but a pod-robot still.

I had had a boyfriend turn into a pod-robot before.

Jackson.

I bolted.

I yanked the twenty-dollar bill from my bag and shoved it at Meghan, saying, "I'll pay you back for the rest, I promise," and blurting out the word *sorry* to Hutch, I ran out of the restaurant and down the block.

In the movies, when a heroine bolts from a difficult situation, the night is black and the empty rain-slicked streets nearly glow. The shot cuts to a few minutes later. She is far from the scene and the people giving her angst, walking picturesquely through the night while some tortured music plays.

But life is not a movie, as I am continually forced to acknowledge, and I stumbled out of Snappy Dragon into sunshine, since in Seattle it doesn't get dark until after nine in the summer. There was no sound track of agonized contemplation, no empty landscape. Instead, there were cars honking and people running errands or going to dinner. Everything looked ordinary and uncinematic.

I ran about a block and then stopped. I had no money for the bus and I had forgotten my house keys. They were in my jacket, draped over the back of a chair in Snappy Dragon.

I was going to have to go back.

I sank to the sidewalk, leaning against a mailbox.

Maybe Noel would run down the street after me.

Was he coming? His coat flapping behind him as he called, "Ruby, wait! Let me explain!"

Was he?

No.

He wasn't coming.

Each minute that passed made it clearer.

It wasn't romantic or intense to have bolted.

It was just mental.

Meghan's Jeep pulled up alongside where I was sitting. She popped the door and called, "I've got your jacket. Get in."

"I'm never leaving this mailbox," I moaned.

"You have to leave the mailbox."

"No, I don't. The mailbox is my only friend. It will protect me against pod-robots and my own lack of sanity. Hello, darling mailbox. You are my savior and protector."

"Leave the mailbox, Roo. I'm your friend."

"'Cause you feel sorry for me. Mailbox doesn't feel sorry for me. Mailbox admires my ambulatory legs and opposable thumbs. Mailbox worships me and will lay down her life for me."

"Roo."

"Mailbox wants you to know that I'm so sorry I left you with the check."

"Oh, shut up!" cried Meghan. "I put it on the credit card. You know my mom pays it for me every month. She never even looks at the bill."

"Seriously? I did not know that, actually."

"Can we have this conversation in the car? Please?"

I sniffed. "Where's Noel?"

"Driving Hutch home."

"Did he say anything about me?"

"He asked if you were okay."

"What did you say?"

"I said obviously you were *not* okay and he should go after you."

"And he said?"

"Will you get in the car, Roo?"

"Do you think he's turned into a pod-robot like Jackson did?"

"No."

"He seemed like a pod-robot. He didn't even hug me."

"Will you just get in the car already?"

"I love you, mailbox. You have been very, very good

to me," I said, patting it. "I will come back and visit you often, even if it means I have to hide from the staff of Snappy Dragon, who will probably pour soup on my head if I ever set foot near their restaurant again."

"Get in!" barked Meghan. "You have ceased to be amusing."

I got in.

The girl had my house keys.

Meghan pulled into traffic and said: "So Noel was all, 'I don't know what to do, I don't know what to do.'"

"What?"

"He sat down at the table and ate a fortune cookie and said he didn't know what to do. Then even Hutch said he should go after you, and Noel put his head down on the table."

"Why?"

"He said, 'I can't deal right now.'" Meghan shrugged. "So I got the check."

Ag.

"I don't know what his problem is," Meghan went on. "He needs to go to boyfriend school."

I sniffed again. "Maybe. But I can't expect him to go running after me when he just got into town and I'm crying like an infant and my parents hate me and I made a scene in the restaurant."

"You can too. He's supposed to go after you if you're upset. Finn would never leave me crying on the street talking to a mailbox."

No. None of Meghan's boyfriends would ever have done that.

"You have bad luck with guys, Roo," Meghan went on. "It's like, you pick ones who have zero talent at being boyfriends."

"Jackson was a good boyfriend."

"Jackson? Please."

"He was a good boyfriend to Kim, at least," I said, "if not to me. He was *capable* of being a good boyfriend."

"Uh, yeah," said Meghan sarcastically. "He cheated on her and then dumped her at school. Roo, hello?"

"Whatever. The problem is obviously me. Guys don't want mental-patient girlfriends. Except in the movies."[2]

Meghan pulled the Jeep into her driveway. "Noel should have gone after you. Even if he wants to break up, he should still have gone after you."

"Maybe," I said, looking at beautiful Meghan in the setting sunlight.

---

[2] Movies where a quality guy loves a girl and sticks with her even though she's one or another kind of insane—maybe alcoholic, maybe addict, maybe psychotic or depressed: *Mad Love, When a Man Loves a Woman, Bed of Roses, Benny and Joon, Eternal Sunshine of the Spotless Mind, 50 First Dates, Almost Famous, Proof, Center Stage, The Hours, My Sassy Girl, What Dreams May Come, Rachel Getting Married, Forrest Gump* (if you consider him a quality guy) and *Betty Blue.* But in real life, I think it's more likely the guy gets sick of the girl's insane behavior and goes off with a nice normal person to live happily ever after. And who can blame him?

Her reddish brown curls hung across her shoulders. She wore a pair of Finn's old jeans and a Tate Prep tank top. Even though I knew most of the girls at school hated her, even though I knew she had lost her dad and saw a shrink, even though she couldn't *really* be as oblivious to pain and weirdness in her heart as she seemed on a day-to-day basis—sometimes I wished I were Meghan instead of me.

Because she never seemed to second-guess her thoughts.

Me, I second-guess everything.

8.

Surprise Kissing!

e-mail from Hutch:

I am eating a strange pretzel in the airport. It is warm, with cinnamon sugar and frosting. Long and thin, not normal pretzel shape. Like the baby of a cinnamon bun and a pretzel.

Seems wrong, somehow.

My flight doesn't leave for another hour.

The real purpose of this e-mail: Are you okay?

I wrote back:

Sorry about last night.

Again, sorry sorry sorry.

Re: Pretzel. That is your last American deliciousness! Savor its American pastry goodness, as from here on in it will be all patisserie.

(You poor thing. Can you tell I am v. jealous?)

Re: Am I okay?

Yeah.

Slept at Meghan's.

Home now.

Mom giving me silent treatment.

I tried to apologize, but she said she wouldn't accept it until I took back what I said about her bossing Dad.

But you know what? She bosses Dad.

So I wouldn't take it back.

Hutch replied:

Re: Last night. No worries. Honestly was relieved not to have to eat white chocolate.

They are boarding my flight now.

I threw the pretzel out and got a giant bag of Sour Patch Kids for last American deliciousness.

Au revoir.

Hutch never wanted to talk about me and Noel. And so we never did. It was almost a forbidden subject between us—not that we ever talked very intimately anyway. Those e-mails were probably some of the most personal things we ever said to each other.

It's funny how you can see a person in your greenhouse every day, and you can watch movies next to him on the couch and sometimes go get pizza or something for most of a summer, and you still don't share all the dark secret details of your lives.

Back when I was friends with Nora, Kim and Cricket, the dark secret details of our lives were what friendship was all about. We talked about fights with our parents, dreams for the future, guys we liked, disappointments and small triumphs. There was an endless series of notes, e-mails and phone calls.

With Hutch, it was all about music and plants and sometimes not talking at all, just existing in the same room together, watching whatever Netflix had just delivered.

There was never a reason to call Hutch twenty minutes after he left my house.

The afternoon after the Snappy Dragon Debacle I worked at the zoo from two until closing. When I was done I changed my clothes, put some minty gum in my mouth and washed the goat smell off my hands, then drove to Noel's house. My hands were shaking on the wheel, but I was determined not to have a panic attack. I found a parking space in front of Noel's place and sat there in the Honda, taking deep breaths and blasting Queen's greatest hits.[1]

---

[1] Go ahead and laugh, but sometimes I listen to Dad's Queen albums even when he and Hutch aren't rocking out in the greenhouse. Okay, and sometimes Guns N' Roses. And sometimes Aerosmith. And once AC/DC.

Retro metal is very good for diverting panic attacks.

A hand knocked on my window.

It was Sydonie, Noel's younger half sister. "Why are you out here?" she wanted to know.

"I came to see your brother."

"Why are you *sitting* out here?"

"I was listening to the song."

"But it's a different song now than it was when you parked," she said.

She had me there.

"You want me to get him?"

"I–"

"I'm going to get him!" cried Sydonie as she ran into the house. "Noelie, Noelie! Your Ruby is here! Your Ruby is here, Noelie!"

Your Ruby.

Your Ruby is here.

I got out of the car and leaned against it, waiting. In a minute, Noel was standing in front of me and in another minute he was kissing me and Sydonie was dancing around us yelling "They're kissing! They're kissing!" and I could feel his arms, warm around my back and then his hand on my cheek and I kissed him back.

"Hey there," Noel said finally.

"Hey yourself," I said. Drunk with the kissing. So surprised. I had been sure he was going to break up with me.

"Sorry I've been hard to reach," he said.

"Oh, that's okay," I told him.

It just popped out of my mouth on impulse–that lie.

It wasn't okay. "Sorry you arrived last night in the middle of my family drama," I added.

Noel kissed me again. "Forget it," he said. "Do you want to go to the movies?"

I nodded. He checked his iPhone for a schedule. "Lots of things will be starting around seven, seven-thirty. You want to just go to the Ave and see what's playing?"

"Okay."

He told Sydonie to tell his parents where he was and got into the Honda.

I couldn't quite believe it.

I seemed to have a boyfriend, after all that.

We went to the Ave and Noel put his hand on my leg while I drove. We got popcorn and saw a movie with a lot of car chases and gunshots. It felt so incredible to hold hands, pressing my forearm against his, rubbing my thumb against his palm. I leaned my head on his shoulder and just breathed in the moment.

Noel was here.

Noel still wanted me.

I told myself I was utterly, completely happy.

⚫

"And?" Doctor Z inquired the next day, looking at me over the rims of her red-framed glasses.

"And what?"

She was silent.

I had never noticed it before, but Doctor Z had a photograph in a frame, facedown on her desk.

Had the photo always been there?

Had I really never noticed it until now?

Was it always facedown?

Like, so her clients couldn't see her top-secret personal photo?

I tried to think whether there had ever been a photograph on her desk.

Did she have children? A dog?

I knew she had a boyfriend named Jonah, because I'd seen them together once, at the Birkenstock store where I used to work.

Maybe the photo was new. Maybe she got a pet, or got engaged to Jonah, or had a baby born in the family.

Whatever it was, it had to be important enough to her that she wanted it up in her workspace even though it meant she had to turn it facedown whenever any of her clients were in there with her, which must be most of the time.

Or maybe it was a gift from a client. Maybe some deranged neurotic thought: Oh, I'm going to give Doctor Z a photo of myself so that she can look at me always. And the client was pretty much loony, so Doctor Z had to display the photo whenever the client came for therapy because otherwise he would go berserk and have to be straightjacketed with maniacal grief. Then when he wasn't there, she didn't really want to look at it, so she turned it facedown.

"Ruby!" Doctor Z startled me.

"What?"

"Is this subject difficult to talk about?"

"I got distracted," I said. "What were we discussing?"

"Your relationship with Noel."

Oh.

Yeah.

Funny how I could forget that, even for a minute. Why is my brain like this? It just switches gears and starts obsessing about something completely unimportant.

"I'm really happy he wants to be together," I told Doctor Z. "It's so great to have him back. I'm so relieved."

She stared at me.

I wasn't lying.

I really felt that way.

I just felt a whole lot of other stuff too.

She stared at me some more. I could hear the clock ticking. I could hear myself breathing. I could hear someone out in the hallway talking.

I twisted my hair. She knew what I was going to say. And she knew I knew she knew.

"But I'm not," I said. "Actually. Happy. Or relieved."

"Why not?"

"I don't know."

"You don't know?"

"Why are people so crap at apologizing?" I said. "I know people feel bad about stuff they've done, but still they don't apologize for it. My dad never apologizes to my mom. He just starts cuddling her or rubbing her shoulders until she stops pouting."

"Could that be a form of apology?"

"Kind of. But also *not.*"

"Noel apologized to you. Didn't you say that he did?"

"Yeah, but 'Sorry I was so hard to reach' isn't a real sorry."

"Why not?"

"He made it sound like the whole thing was out of his control. He didn't say, 'Sorry I didn't call you back. Sorry I didn't write you. Sorry I hurt your feelings. Sorry I didn't run after you.'"

"It didn't feel like a real sorry," Doctor Z said. She does that a lot. Repeats what I've said.

"And when he said sorry he was hard to reach, I said, 'It's okay.' But only because that's what you're *supposed* to say when someone says sorry. Not because I meant it."

"Uh-huh."

"Or maybe because I *wished* it was okay. But—"

She looked at me.

"—it was a complete lie."

"Oh."

"I was basically acting fake the whole night, trying to pretend I was just letting everything go. Or like I hadn't even minded how he'd disappeared on me and not called me and all that. Like I was some extra-mellow relaxed girlfriend who didn't care about anything. Like those two poems made up for everything." I bit my nails. "I kept thinking—all night I kept thinking that if I had never gone over to his house after work, he might never have even called me."

"Really?"

"He would have just gone about his life, avoiding me, or forgetting about me, or meaning to call me but not just yet–whatever he's been doing since halfway through the New York trip."

"Mm." Doctor Z popped a piece of Nicorette out of its packaging and put it thoughtfully in her mouth. "What did you two talk about?"

I shrugged. "The movie we saw. Whether or not Christian Bale is deranged. Why there aren't more female action heroes."

"Ah."

"Why did we have to go to a movie? For once in my life, I didn't want to go to a movie."

"No?"

"We didn't talk that much, even."

"Oh."

Noel and I had kissed in the front seat of the Honda when I drove him home, and we had held hands in the theater–but whenever I spoke I had this sense that I was chattering at him. Like some part of his brain was elsewhere.

He wasn't truly listening. So I didn't tell him anything.

You have to have someone listening if you're going to really talk.

9.

The Waketastic Adventure!

a video clip:

Roo's parents sit on their couch. Polka-dot is there too, his head on Elaine's lap. Kevin has garden dirt on his T-shirt. Elaine is wearing black, her frizzy hair puffed out around her head.

> *Roo: (behind the camera) What's your definition of friendship?*
>
> *Elaine: I don't know why we're doing this, Kevin. She still hasn't taken back what she said. I told you I wasn't outputting energy toward her until I had a full apology.*
>
> *Kevin: It's for her college applications. We agreed to be supportive of her college applications, even*

though the two of you are going through a difficult time.

Elaine: It's not a difficult time. She just owes me an apology. (Looking directly at the camera.) That's what friendship is, Ruby. Apologizing when you know you should.

Roo: I did apologize.

Elaine: Not fully. I don't know why we have so much trouble being friends. A mother and a daughter should be the closest friends.

Kevin: My mother and I weren't friends. She was my mother. She mothered me.

Elaine: Are you saying something about my mothering?

Kevin: No.

A couple of days before school started, Meghan was with Finn per usual and I didn't have to work at the zoo and Noel had to go shopping with his stepdad for school clothes and cross-country shoes, so I helped Dad in the greenhouse a bit and then went out on the dock to mess with the video camera.

I was trying to figure out how to shoot something dark with sunlight behind it, fiddling around with settings and playing snippets back to see how my shots turned out, when I heard the putt-putt of a motorboat.

"Did you run out of gas again?" I shouted when Gideon was twenty feet away.

"No," he yelled. "I'm full."

"Do you need a Band-Aid?"

"No." He cut the engine and tied up.

"What do you need?"

"A driver." He climbed out and bopped me on the arm, dude style.

"What?"

"You ever wakeboard?"

I rolled my eyes.

"But you water-ski." He said it like a statement.

No. I didn't. I mean, I had been out on the Van Deusens' boat before while other people were water-skiing, the summer after freshman year, but the one time I tried to actually get up on water skis I had fallen flat on my butt within two seconds.

"Hasn't Evergreen started yet?" I said, to change the subject.

Gideon wasn't fooled. "Yeah, but it's the weekend. Okay, so you don't water-ski. But aren't you some kind of awesome swimmer?"

"I'm on the team at Tate," I said. "But I'm not taking home a lot of ribbons."

"It'll be easy for you," he said. "And driving the boat's really fun. No roads. Nothing but the wind on your face."

Was I really going out on a boat with Gideon Van Deusen?

When I completely had a boyfriend?

"I'll teach you," said Gideon, smiling. "Wakeboarding is actually easier than waterskiing for a lot of people."

"Um. I gotta ask my dad," I said. "Will you wait here?"

"Sure." Gideon immediately lay down on the dock. "I'll just absorb some sun."

I went into the house, but I didn't ask my dad. He was mumbling something about his mother into a dried-out peony plant. What I did was call Noel.

He hadn't called me that day, or the day before. I hadn't seen him since Thursday night.

The cell went to voice mail.

I tried again.

Again voice mail.

The third time I left a message. "Hey, it's Ruby. You want to go get ice cream with me tonight? I have a craving for Mix. Maybe coffee with Heath bar and chocolate chips. Call me right now if you can go."

Then I sat on my bed and waited for him to call me back.

And waited.

And he didn't call.

I don't know why I was surprised.

I put on a bathing suit. The Speedo my parents got me for team practice, nothing cute.

And still, I sat on my bed.

And still, the phone didn't ring.

I put on a cotton vintage skirt and a T-shirt. Flip-flops.

I grabbed a towel.

I looked at the phone.

Noel was my boyfriend. But he wasn't my real live boyfriend anymore.

Fine.

The water was insanely cold, and it took me five tries to get up on the wakeboard. When I did, my legs felt like jelly and the sun was in my eyes–but I was up, and light was glinting on the water, and I was cutting in and back across the wake of the boat, and I was laughing and screaming both together and it was just gorgeous. The universe seemed golden for a minute.

Then I was over my head in the bitter water, and Gideon was steering the boat around to pick me up, and he was laughing. "Don't stick your butt out! The moment you stick your butt out it's over."

He reached his tan arm down and I grabbed it and he hauled me up onto the boat. "You wanna go again?"

I nodded.

So I went again.

And again.

And then it was a long time before I fell.

I drove for a while, and Gideon attempted numerous tricks, many of which failed. He was trying to get airborne, but most of the time he just crashed into the water, laughing. When he got tired, we floated for a while. I was cold and he gave me his fleece hoodie to wear. We drank Cokes from a cooler and ate these weird organic cheese puffs Gideon brought.

I thought, and not for the first time, that Gideon would make an excellent boyfriend. As I watched him driving the motorboat back toward my dock, I said to myself:

This is Gideon, whom I loved in sixth grade. This is Gideon, who doesn't live in the Tate Universe. This is Gideon, who traveled the world for a year after high school.

This is Gideon, who plays guitar. This is Gideon, whose leg touched mine all through the movie that time. This is Gideon, who listens to what I say.

This is Gideon, straightforward and normal.

This is Gideon, who said I should call him if I didn't have a boyfriend.

"Thanks for the waketastic adventure," I told him.

He looked down at me. "You're . . ."

"What?"

Gideon shook his head. "Different from most of Nora's friends, that's all."

More deranged, I thought. "I'm not sure we're exactly friends anymore." Nora had been on Decatur Island with her parents since a week after the funeral, so I hadn't seen her. I wasn't sure what the status was.

"She said you guys made up."

"She did?"

"Yeah."

"Then I guess we did," I said.

Gideon ate a cheese puff. "Cricket and Kim and that new one, Katarina what'shername—"

"Dolgen."

"And Heidi and Ariel. They're all the same."

I didn't know what he was talking about. They all seemed so unique to me. Especially Cricket and Kim. They had been my closest friends for years and years. "We should probably change the subject," I said.

"Okay." We didn't speak. The roar of the boat made it nearly impossible to have a conversation anyway.

As I got out of the boat, I took off Gideon's hoodie and gave it back to him. "Thanks for letting me borrow this."

"Keep it."

"What? No, I can't."

"Just for now," Gideon said. "I don't need it for the drive home."

"But I have sweatshirts in the house," I said. "I don't need it either."

Gideon jumped into the boat and started the engine. "Keep it," he repeated, over the noise. "This way, I have to come get it back from you."

Noel and I did go get ice cream that night. It was okay. It just seemed like he was—not a pod-robot, but maybe a recent lobotomy patient. Like part of his brain had been cut out by surgeons in an experimental procedure that left him with only a section of his former personality intact.[1]

Either that, or he didn't like me that much anymore.

I tried to ask him about it, but the conversation just went like this.

> *Roo: Hey. Um. Is there anything wrong?*
> *Noel: What?*
> *Roo: Is there anything wrong?*
> *Noel: No.*
> *Roo: It seems like something's wrong between us.*
> *Noel: I don't know what you're talking about.*
>   *Everything's fine.*

So I shut up and ate my ice cream. Then later, Noel stopped his mom's car in front of my dock, and he seemed so cold. Like he was just expecting me to hop out, without a kiss goodnight or anything. This huge awkwardness loomed between us, and I freaked out a little and couldn't help but break one of Meghan's rules

---

[1] Lobotomies: For real, they used to do this to people from the 1930s to the '50s. Just chopped out a bit of the brain to see if it solved a person's mental health problems, including anxiety disorders and just inconvenient behavior like moodiness or defiance. The procedures involved either drilling holes in the scalp or going in through the eye with an ice pick. And get this: the doctor didn't need to get the patient's informed consent, so you could completely just go to bed in the mental hospital and wake up with a section of your brain having been removed.

Needless to say, it's good I wasn't born back then, or I'd have had an ice pick through the eyeball ages ago.

for what to talk about when you're alone in the dark with your boyfriend.

> *Roo: What are you thinking?*
> *Noel: Until a minute ago I was thinking about parallel*
>   *parking.*
> *Roo: So everything's okay?*
> *Noel: Yeah.*
> *Roo: Things seem a little odd is all.*
> *Noel: They do?*
> *Roo: It's hard to talk to you.*
> *Noel: I don't know what you mean.*
> *Roo: You don't think anything's wrong?*
> *Noel: Nothing's wrong, Ruby.*
> *Roo: Forget it, then.*

I was about to get out of the car when he leaned in and put his hand on my boob. He didn't even kiss me first. It was like the least romantic boob fondle in the history of all boob fondling. I might even go so far as to call it a grope.

Actually, if he hadn't been my boyfriend I would have slapped his hand away and called him a Neanderthal. As it was, I let him grope it. Then we kissed goodnight for a while, but all the time I was thinking: Excuse me, but that's *my* boob; it's not yours to just grab because you want a conversation to be over.

While we were kissing, I could tell Noel was really

getting into it—you know, in the nether regions—and I was wondering how a guy could want to make out with me so much—he was all over me, really—and still not *call* me the way he used to, or send me e-mails, or even really talk to me when I was trying to have a serious conversation. I didn't really touch him back, the way I usually did, because my brain was going:

Why do you say nothing's wrong when there's obviously something wrong?

And if you don't like me that much anymore, why do you like grabbing my boob?

In fact, I think you like grabbing my boob more now than you did before you left.

And oh, actually, that feels amazing.

And oh, I think I love you.

I do love you, Noel.

At least, I love the you who *used* to be here.

But now, that you is somewhere else.

Like maybe New York City.

Or maybe just closed off to me.

And was it something I did?

Or something I said?

And oh, that neck-kissing thing is—

No one ever did exactly that before.

I do love you.

But hello, I don't really feel like kissing when everything's so weird with us.

And I don't know if you get to touch my boobs and

kiss my neck that way when you wait so long to call me back and you never seem to hear what I am trying to tell you.

It was really quite a complicated situation to be in, and not anywhere near as fun as getting horizontal had been, back when everything was cheerful and simple between us. Eventually when his hand roamed up my dress toward my butt, I pulled away and said, "Something's wrong with *me,* then, Noel, if nothing's wrong with you."

He crinkled his forehead. "What?" It was like he'd forgotten the whole conversation we'd just been having.

I didn't want to repeat myself. "I have to go," I said.

"Ruby, wait!" he called as I got out of the car. "Are you mad?"

"No," I turned. "I just have to go. We have school tomorrow."

Noel didn't get out of the car. He didn't chase after me. Just like at Snappy Dragon, he didn't chase after me.

10.

An Agonizing Public Scene! With Violence!

a video clip: Meghan, leaning against the front of her Jeep, which is parked in front of the Olivers' dock. She's holding her usual thermos full of vanilla cappuccino and wearing a golf team T-shirt, a jean skirt and Birkenstocks.

> Roo: (behind the camera) It's the first day of school, so
>   I want to ask you about popularity.
> Meghan: I used to think I was popular, and then later
>   I realized I wasn't.
> Roo: What do you mean?
> Meghan: Back when I was going out with Bick. He was a
>   senior, and he had all these friends, and we went to
>   lots of parties. I hung around with all these senior
>   girls. I thought I was popular.
> Roo: Then what?

Meghan: *You didn't invite me to your Spring Fling party, remember?*

Roo: *I'm so sorry.*

Meghan: *Well, I was upset at first, but then I realized. I had been to all these other parties, all year, but no one had* ever *invited me. I just went. Because Bick was invited. In fact, not one of those people I ate lunch with every day* ever called me. *Or e-mailed me. Or put a note in my mail cubby. I never saw them if Bick wasn't around.*

Roo: *Ag.*

Meghan: *I know. Then you and Nora started actually calling me, and we were like, friends for real and went to the B&O and wrote in your notebook and hung around on the weekends. I thought—Oh. Those people, all those seniors, they aren't my friends. They were never my friends. So actually I'm more popular now than I was when I went to all those parties.*

Roo: *You feel popular now?*

Meghan: *Sure.*

Roo: *But I'm a complete roly-poly. Being friends with me is like the opposite of popularity.*

Meghan: *Get over it, Roo. If you have friends who actually like you, you're popular enough.*

When school started, Mom was barely speaking to me. Since her Snappy Dragon duck temptation, she had started buying and eating cooked food—not to please me, but because she had practically been starving herself for a year eating only things like celery juice and peanut goulash. She was probably ten pounds under her natural weight and had a serious hunger buildup. I came home one day to find her heating up barbecued ribs in the oven and mashing potatoes.

After that, one of the ways she punished me for speaking my mind was by continually cooking meat. I'm a vegetarian, not because I think humans shouldn't ever eat meat so much as because freshman year I read an article in the Sunday magazine about the way these big meat companies treat the animals, penning them up so they can't even turn around or lie down, feeding them foods that aren't natural to their bodies, injecting them with massive amounts of hormones and antibiotics, just horrible stuff. I couldn't stand it, so I stopped eating meat.[1]

Anyway, Mom bought an enormous book on charcuterie and a cookbook claiming to be the ultimate American barbecue bible. She started talking about buying a grass-fed cow, having it professionally slaughtered, and smoking and curing the meat herself. She was reading a lot of blogs on the subject, subscribed to a publication called *Meat Paper,* and researched jumbo-sized freezers that might fit on our northern deck.

---

[1] I still eat things with eggs and dairy in them, not because it doesn't upset me the way *those* are produced (it does), but because I'm not perfect. Also, my quest for deliciousness, especially in the form of baked goods, makes it pretty much impossible to say goodbye to butter. But maybe I'll give it up when I'm older and more mature.

Most nights of the week, she was roasting something sizable and dead in the oven and planning to serve it with nothing but a green vegetable. So I was still getting nothing but vegetables for dinner, though at least they were cooked, and I had to stare at a large hunk of dead animal on the table every evening.

My father, however, ate like he'd just been released from prison, shoveling chicken legs into his mouth and sucking all the meat off them.

"You'll crack eventually, Ruby," said my mother. "Tomorrow I'm making Swedish-style meatballs with veal, beef and pork. All three! I'll serve them over rice."

"I'm not going to crack for *veal*," I told her. "Veal is the most unethical meat you can eat. Besides, are you really interested in being a carnivore, or is this all about making me crack?"

"It's not all about making you crack," said Mom smugly. "I just think you will."

Back to the first day of school. It was weird to be a senior. The new herd of freshmen looked like frightened deer. The junior boys were taller than before summer. Meghan and I sat at the senior tables near the big windows of the refectory, just like all the seniors had for countless years before us. It felt surreal and powerful.

The strangest thing was being at school without Jackson. Ever since he'd come back from Japan my sophomore year, even before we'd started going out and long after we'd broken up, I'd had Jackson radar. I'd known where he was standing, noticed what he was wearing and wondered what he was talking about, every single day.

Now Jackson was at Cornell, three thousand miles away, and I would never have to wonder if he was looking at me, or *not* looking at me, or ignoring me, or hating me, or lusting after me. Not ever again.

Nora had her camera slung around her neck and was snapping first-day pictures of all her friends. She took one of me standing outside the main building and told me to have a good first day of school. I was glad to see her, and felt more relaxed since Gideon had told me *she* told *him* we'd made up—but nothing felt the same as it had before we argued. We weren't starting senior year *together*.

Kim had a supershort haircut that made her look mod and adult. Cricket's summer at drama school had led her to go heavy on the eye makeup and black clothes. Ariel Olivieri, who made out with Noel last year and was therefore another person I was destined to have plugged into my radar, had spent the summer perfecting her tan.

I wondered if I looked different to them after a couple of months away. I had on jeans, Converse and a vintage bowling shirt. I didn't dress up because I was trying to look like I didn't care—you know, about the first day of school, how I looked, what people might be saying about me—but when I looked in the bathroom mirror I thought maybe I was trying too hard. To not care.

I put on lip gloss.

Then rubbed it off.

I shouldn't have trimmed my bangs myself.

Varsha and Spencer from swim team ran up to me by the mail cubbies. I hadn't seen them all summer, except once when I'd run into them at Pike Place Market and we all got cinnamon rolls. They weren't my real friends. They were swim team friends. They were Future Doctors of America. I didn't find them fantastically amusing, but they were neither catty nor golden and at least they didn't seem to hate me or think I was a slut. "We're counting on you for the relay," Varsha told me. "Now that Angelica graduated, you'll swim backstroke. Sound good?"

"Spankin'," I said.

"Huh?"

"Excellent. If Wallace says okay," I told them. "Though Laura's faster than me."

"Nah," said Spencer. "She's got a boyfriend. She barely worked out all summer. You worked out, right?"

"In August. But I was pretty out of shape when I started. I didn't even play lacrosse last spring."

"Why not?" Varsha asked.

"No way I'd make varsity goalie with Chelsea Lefferts still here, so I bailed. Spring was a complete slugfest."

"Slugfest!" laughed Spencer. "You say the strangest things, Ruby. Doesn't she, Varsha? Anyway, it doesn't matter. We're going to be the hottest relay team."

That was how conversations with Varsha and

Spencer went, and they kind of filled me with ennui. Still, I was grateful they were so nice, because I had been angsting about lunch. Now I knew I could eat with the swim team girls. Meghan was likely to spend lunch at Finn's table of soccer muffins[2] (who were all about Dude Time and therefore made me uncomfortable and also bored), Hutch was in Paris and Nora was pretty certain to be at Cricket and Kim's table this year.

And Noel. He was the sort of person who was welcome anywhere. A floater. Last year, before we were going out, he sometimes sat with guys from the cross-country team, sometimes with a bunch of sophomore girls, sometimes with us and sometimes with people he knew from art class or November Week. It was hard to say where he'd be for sure, and if he was with people I didn't know that well, I wasn't sure how it would feel to just go and sit down next to him.

Oh.

Ag.

I had just wondered whether or not I'd be welcome to sit with Noel in the refectory.

He was absolutely not my real live boyfriend anymore.

I mean, I knew that. But this was proof upon proof.

What was wrong?

How had we gone from love to *this*?

109

---

[2] Muffin: Bland person. Mildly pleasant, but lacking in spice, novelty and deliciousness.

I was thinking all through first-period Calc, second-period Physics and third-period Women Writers. Each time I had to walk from class to class, I wondered if I'd run into Noel and how things would be between us since I'd jumped out of the car last night.

Was he mad?

Was I mad?

Could we talk about it, or would it just be a replay of the same conversation, where he insisted nothing was wrong?

Maybe I should just pretend everything was perfect. That seemed to be what he wanted.

But everything wasn't perfect.

It wasn't.

Did I really want to be fake with Noel, of all people?

After Women Writers, I went to the top of the math building for my College Application Process Workshop—CAP. All seniors had this on their schedule once a week in the fall. It was supposed to be an information-sharing process where we met in groups of ten to give each other support on our applications, recommend schools we'd researched and so on.

Dittmar (the college admissions guy) had cleared space on the rug in his office and was sitting on it cross-legged. His madras pants hiked up in this position to reveal hairy pink legs and sweat socks. "Ruby, sit down," he said, smiling and tapping his clipboard happily.

Noel, Kim and Cricket were there already, sitting across from each other. So was Ariel Olivieri (who had kissed Noel), Darcy the Neanderthal and several Future Doctors of America.

I hadn't known Noel would be there.

He met my eyes, so I sat by him.

I mean, to *not* sit by him when he was my boyfriend would have been weird. Plus if I didn't sit by him, I'd be sitting close to Kim and Cricket, which was impossible. "Hi," I whispered as I eased myself down onto the carpet. "Sorry I freaked out yesterday."

Noel nodded, but he didn't answer. He was looking at some Xerox the Ditz had handed out.

It would have been nice if he'd said, "That's okay, Ruby. I understand. I don't mind if you freak out on me every now and then"—but I wasn't going to push it.

The sleeves of Noel's canvas jacket were frayed and his fingernails were bitten and red. I could hear him wheezing slightly and wondered if he had his puffer in his pocket, and whether he'd have to leave class to use it.

Dittmar handed me a stack of papers. *Tate Prep College Advisement Wants to Know All About YOU!* it said on the top. *From your parents, from your friends and from Y-O-U YOU! Please take the time to fill out the questionnaire below so we can best assist YOU in finding the right colleges to which you should apply.*

As the rest of the students came in and sat down, I flipped through the pages. Inside were the expected questions about extracurricular activities, religious activities, awards, honors, sports. Dittmar wanted to know our favorite book and our proposed field of study. Also things about whether we wanted to go to an urban or rural school, a college or a university, large or small, private or state, blah blah blah.

After that was a parent questionnaire.

How do you see your child?

What kind of education do you want for your child?

What are your child's strengths and weaknesses?

As if we were four years old.

Last was a sheet that Dittmar explained we were supposed to give to a peer. "Sometimes a friend will come up with ideas for what you can put on your application that you never would think of," he enthused. "So pick a friend and have him or her write some answers. You'll be surprised what insights your pals have that can help you in your pursuit of higher education!"

I passed the friend questionnaire to Noel. Like a peace offering, after what had happened last night. He took it, and while the Ditz rambled on, I stared at him. Noel's profile was sharp and beautiful, like he'd been drawn with a single fluid line of ink. I looked at his pale, white skin and the slight line of chapping underneath his bottom lip and felt so, so lucky to have touched them.

We had to fix things. Somehow.

We had to.

I loved him.

But I didn't know what to do.

Noel wrote a note on the back of his questionnaire packet. *I have something to ask you.*

I wrote back. *What?*

Did he finally want to know why I'd been upset last night?

Did he want—

"Take a moment and close your eyes," said Dittmar. "Picture yourself at college. Picture the dining hall. Picture the grounds. Picture the dorm rooms. Picture yourself in the library. Picture *you,* doing the extracurricular activities of your choice."

I opened my eyes midspeech. The Ditz was reading from a piece of paper.

"Ruby, please close your eyes," he scolded. "It's essential to fully visualize yourself at college for this to work."

I closed my eyes.

"Cricket," said the Ditz. "Now *your* eyes are open. Didn't you hear what I just said to Ruby?"

"No," said Cricket. "I was visualizing."

"Well, visualize some more," said Dittmar. "We're visualizing for two minutes. And there are forty-three seconds left. Now forty. Now— There. Thank you, Cricket."

I opened my eyes. With great stealth. And looked at what Noel had written.

Did you go out with Nora's brother Gideon? it said on the paper.

Ag! Ag and more ag!

Ag ag ag ag.

Noel was angry at me.

I could see that now. I could see it in the set of his mouth.

How did he find out?

Why hadn't I told him?

Why had I set foot on that boat?

Stupid, stupid me.

What had I done?

"Time's up!" said Dittmar.

"No," I told Noel out loud.

It was true.

But it was also not true.

Noel wrote some more as Dittmar began speaking. *I was in line this morning to fix my schedule with the registrar. Nora and Heidi were in front of me,* he scribbled. Dittmar was going around the circle asking people what they'd seen with their eyes shut. *I was a few people back and they were talking so they didn't see me,* wrote Noel. *Nora told Heidi that Gideon came down to Seattle from Evergreen in order to take you out.*

I read the paper with a sinking feeling in my chest. *Not true,* I wrote.

Then why would Nora say that? She didn't even know I was behind her.

The girl next to me had just finished describing herself riding horses and doing some mad partying at college.

"You'll want a rural school," said the Ditz. "Are you considering an agricultural program?"

The girl looked at him blankly. "I just like to ride."

Dittmar sighed. "Okay. I'll make a note of that. Now, Ruby. What's on your mind?"

"Noel, why are you jealous all the time?" I cried.

I didn't mean to say that. I meant to answer Dittmar about New York City, Philadelphia, Los Angeles–living in a big city and making movies. I felt my face burn.

"What?" Noel looked shocked.

"You were jealous of me and Jackson last spring, now you're jealous of me and Gideon."

He looked startled.

Dittmar intervened. "Ruby, let's leave our personal issues outside my office, shall we?"

"Ugh," jeered Cricket. "She's always making a scene of some kind. Like any of us is interested in your dramas, Ruby."

I didn't think she was interested in my dramas. I just couldn't myself be interested in anything else at the moment. "Why don't you just believe that you're the one I want and trust me?" I asked Noel. I had to have it out with him–whatever it was that had gone all wrong between us.

Noel didn't answer.

"Ruby!" Dittmar's voice was sharp. "Are you ready to share your college visualization with us? Or shall I come back to you when you've collected your temper?"

"Is it because of all the stuff written on the bathroom walls about me?" I asked. "The things people whisper behind my back? Because I know what they say. 'Slut.' 'Tart.' 'I hear she goes on her knees behind the gymnasium.' I've heard all of it since sophomore year, but I thought you didn't believe it."

"I don't," said Noel quietly. But I wasn't sure he was telling the truth.

"Listen," I said. "You would never, ever have anything to worry about if you would just *call* me, and come over to my house for no reason like you used to, or else have a real conversation and tell me why everything's changed. You'd never have to worry about Gideon or anyone else. If you'd just look at me the way you used to, so I could *talk* to you–"

Noel tossed his head. "*If.* That's the word there."

"What do you mean?"

"*If.* You said *if* I'd do x, y, whatever it is you want, *then* I could trust you. But apparently I haven't done those things to your satisfaction, so then what? I can't trust you?"

I wanted to tell him he could.

I wanted to be the girl who had never flirted with Gideon, never thought he'd make a better boyfriend than Noel.

But I wasn't. I had done those things.

"You're so suspicious," I said. "The only reason I even went anywhere with Gideon was because you didn't call me back. You hadn't called me in three days when he came over."

"So you did go out with him."

"He wanted to go wakeboarding. He pulled up at my dock. It wasn't a plan."

"Nora said he came down specially."

"I don't know anything about that. He made it

sound like one of his friends had bailed on him or something and he needed a driver."

Noel shook his head. "I can't believe you, Ruby."

"It wasn't anything. He taught me to wakeboard and we ate cheese puffs."

"Then why wouldn't you tell me about it?" Noel asked. "Why would you *not tell me you learned to wakeboard* if you didn't feel guilty about it? It's not like that's a completely uneventful part of your day."

He had a point.

Of course I had felt guilty.

Of course that was why I hadn't told him.

Suddenly, I looked around me. I was standing in the center of Dittmar's office, revealing my ugly, unfaithful heart to everyone there. Confirming every rotten thing anyone had ever said or thought about me.

"Ruby!" It was Kim. "We're trying to deal with our college applications. This is really important to everyone here but you. So will you please leave?"

Dittmar scribbled something on a sheet of paper. "To the headmaster, both of you. Go, now. And don't bring this personal agony back into my office. Ever. Again."

"I can't tell you *anything* since you got back from New York," I said to Noel as I snatched the piece of paper from Dittmar. "You don't react. You don't have anything to say. It's like talking to a lobotomy patient."

He looked at me silently.

"That came out wrong," I said.

"Yeah. I bet."

I grabbed my bag and left the office. As I headed down the spiral steps of the math building, I could hear Noel's footsteps behind me.

"It's like you don't care anymore, Noel," I yelled up into the stairwell. "That's what it feels like. And I've tried and tried to talk to you about it, but the not-caring means you don't want to hear what I have to say about it, and then—"

"Would I be mad about you going out with Gideon if I didn't care?" called Noel. I kept running down the stairs.

"I didn't go out with him!" I called back. "Nothing happened."

A mathematical-looking freshman nearly collided with me as I rounded the landing. She squeaked and ran down the hall to her class.

"Stop being jealous!" I went on, yelling up to Noel.

And what I meant was:

Believe in me.

Don't listen to what people say.

Don't read the writing on the walls.

You, of all people.

Believe in me.

I kept stumbling down the stairs, but Noel ran cross-country and he caught me easily. He grabbed my upper arm. "Won't you just listen?" he said, his voice taut.

"Don't grab me," I said. "You don't get to grab me like that."

He didn't let go. "It is so unfair," he said, "to accuse me of not caring and then harsh on me for being jealous."

Okay.

I could see that.

But you know what?

Through this whole argument he hadn't said he cared.

He'd said, "Would I be mad about you going out with Gideon if I didn't care?"

But not that he *actually cared.*

"Jealousy is not the kind of caring I want," I said. "And stop grabbing me."

"How can I trust you when you're going out with other people behind my back?"

"Not other people. One other person."

"One is enough."

"You're not really here," I told him. "You're not my real live boyfriend."

"I'm not your boyfriend?"

"That's not what I meant. I meant, you're not acting like a boyfriend. Not a real live one. Not like the ones Meghan has."

"I don't know what you think one should act like!" Noel was shouting, and his voice echoed up the staircase.

"Will you please stop grabbing me?" I said.

"This isn't making me happy," Noel said, without letting go. "I came back from New York and I thought you would make me happy but I'm not happy."

"Are we breaking up, then?"

Noel didn't answer.

"Are we breaking up?" I repeated.

When he didn't answer again, I couldn't stand it.

"If you're not going to answer, then what you mean is yes," I said. I reached for his fingers, still holding my arm, and pulled them off me by force. I threw his hand away from me. "Let me go."

Noel was wheezing, and maybe he was dizzy—I don't know—but he lost his balance as I pushed his arm and fell down half a flight of stairs. Not head over heels, like in the movies, but awkwardly, like he was made of paper, crumpling, and like his backpack weighed more than he did. He landed on his knees with a crack.

"Shit, oh, shit," he moaned.

I looked down at him. On his hands and knees, almost like a prayer. Breathing funny.

Had I pushed him?

Not quite.

He'd been grabbing me.

But had I pushed him, really?

A little bit. Not down the stairs but away from me. Yes, I had pushed him.

I stumbled down. "Are you okay?"

"Just go away," said Noel, not meeting my eyes. "I'm fine, everything's fine, just go away."

"Do you need your puffer? Are your knees hurt?"

"I'm fine," he said again. "Just leave me."

"But—"

"Leave me," he said bitterly.

And so I did.

I skipped lunch and went straight to the gym, where I got undressed and stood in the shower stall under the hot water, letting tears and shampoo stream down my face.

"I have an idea for a business," Mom announced at dinner a week later. She had barely been speaking to me in the wake of the Snappy Dragon Debacle. I ignored her as much as possible too, because even though I knew I'd acted badly, I felt she was acting worse. She didn't seem to care that my father was miserable, or that my heart was broken.

Anyway, we did all sit down to dinner together most nights, even though none of us had anything to say—Dad 'cause he was depressed and Mom and me 'cause we didn't like each other anymore—but this night she suddenly wanted to communicate.

"I think we can get investors for it," Mom said, shoveling a piece of steak into her mouth, "and I scouted a location down in Pioneer Square. The rent is ten thousand dollars a month, but for sure we'll make a profit in the first year because there is nothing like this in Seattle. Nothing. And people are gonna love it."

At the phrase "ten thousand dollars a month" my dad choked on a mouthful. "What's the idea?"

"Pioneer Square is the best neighborhood for it," Mom went on, ignoring him. "Because you get the tourist trade there as well as locals."

"You're looking at places to rent already?" Dad asked. "What's the idea?"

"I started drawing up a business plan too," Mom said. "You know I have to do more than copyediting when Ruby goes to college. If she doesn't get a full scholarship, we're going to need every penny I can possibly earn."

"And you think a good plan for earning that money is to sign a lease for ten thousand dollars a month?"

"It's not like *you're* earning much," snapped Mom. "Since your mother passed, you haven't finished your Web site, you haven't written any newspaper columns, you haven't–"

"What's your idea, Mom?" I interrupted.

"A meatloafery," she said.

"What is that?"

"A restaurant," said my mother.[3] "With brick ovens the way they have at fancy pizza places, so you can see into them and watch the meatloaves cooking."

Dad put down his fork and looked at her in astonishment.

"People come in," Mom went on, "and on their table is an assortment of ground meats, different kinds of bread crumbs–like maybe garlic bread, rye, pumpernickel–and

---

[3] Perhaps I should note here that my mother has no culinary training, no business experience and, apparently, no sense of her own limitations.

ingredients in pretty little dishes. Ketchup, barbecue sauce, onions, roasted garlic, maybe Dijon mustard, maybe chopped tomato."

"Back up," I told her. "An assortment of ground meats?"

"Of course," said Mom. "I'm thinking lamb, pork, veal, beef and turkey to start. Then we can have chicken and buffalo, too, once business picks up. Buffalo meat is very current."

"Just raw on the table?"

"Sure. How else are people going to make their own meatloaf? The best meatloaves are a mix of meats. You would know that if you'd tried the one I made on Sunday and looked at the cookbook like I asked you."

"I'm a vegetarian," I reminded her.

Mom went on, ignoring me. "At MeatMix we'll be letting people choose the mix they're in the mood for!"

"MeatMix?"

"That's the name of the restaurant. Or maybe MoodMeat. Or maybe KitLoaf? Juana thought of KitLoaf." She took a drink from her wineglass.

"You're going to have hygiene issues," I told her. "All those people mixing up raw meat."

"We'll have rubber gloves," said Mom. "So people can actually mix with their hands. That's half the fun of making meatloaf, feeling it squish between your fingers. It's not the same if you use a spatula." She stood up to clear the table.

"Meatloaf takes an hour to cook," said Dad, as if

coming out of a stupor. "What are people going to do while they wait for their food?"

"There's going to be a full bar!" snapped my mother, as if he were an idiot. "People will bond. They'll talk over recipes and give each other tips."

"Not everyone is as into meatloaf as you are," Dad cautioned.

"Comfort food is a new trend in restaurants," Mom said.

"Are they gonna eat in the same place they cooked?" I wanted to know. "Like on a table covered with scraps of raw meat?"

"An hour is a long time to wait for your meal," Dad said. "I don't know if just drinks will cut it. Isn't this a family kind of place?"

"If you're letting kids in there, the hygiene issues are going to be even more serious," I argued. "What if they get snot in their meatloaf? What if they drool? Are you really going to just stick a snot meatloaf in the oven and serve it to a customer? Even if it's the customer's own snot?"

"I'm not certain you're going to find investors for this, Elaine," my dad said gently.

"Why are you two so unsupportive?" Mom exploded. "All I do is support, support, support both of you, all the time!"

"It's ten thousand dollars a month," said Dad. "In the year before we send Ruby to college."

"This kind of attitude is just what I'm talking about!" she cried. "You can't even imagine for a single second that something of mine is going to be a success, can you? You can't think that it might make money and *pay* for Ruby's damn college."

"It's a meatloafery," I said. "You're not even a chef."

"It's *make your own!*" she said, stamping her feet.

"Elaine," said Dad, in a pleading tone of voice. "I'm not trying to be unsupportive. I–"

"You're cutting me down!" said Mom. "Neither of you lets me even finish explaining my business plan. You think you're so quick, so clever, making me feel stupid. But is that a positive way to deal with other people? Is it?"

I knew she was partly right. But she was so unsympathetic. She was living with two broken people, two people deep in the pain of Reginald.[4] My grandmother was dead. My true love had turned cold. Dad's mother was gone. And Mom acted like our sadness was one big irritant: an obstacle in her quests for smoked meat, yogic enlightenment and performance-art fame.

"I'm cutting you down because it's a stupid idea," I told her.

The rest of the evening did not go well.

125

---

4 Reginald is what Doctor Z and I call the grieving process, or a process of accepting the difficult things that have happened. Because phrases like *grieving process* make me throw up a little bit in my mouth.

11

The Wenchery of Cricket and Kim!

Parent Questionnaire
Please fill this form out as soon as possible so we can begin helping your child in his or her college applications process.

How do you see your child?
As little as possible.

What kind of education do you want for your child?
One that doesn't require me to fill out stupid questionnaires. Also, one that's free.

What are your child's strengths and weaknesses?
Ruby is self-involved and neurotic. She may be a repressed lesbian. She may be an anorexic.

As for strengths: she is superb at making stingingly unkind remarks.

From your observation, what subjects is your child most interested in?
Staring at the television. Moping. Acting superior.

What is your educational background, and that of your spouse?
Nothing that prepared us in any way for the horrors of raising a teenager.

—written with black Sharpie in my mom's large, loopy cursive on Dittmar's printout.

My senior year went on.
Without Noel.
Without Noel.
I worked at the zoo.
I did a lot of homework.
I swam after school.
Without Noel.
I sent away for college applications.
I walked Polka-dot.
I went to therapy.
Without Noel.
Doing all these things, I cried a lot.
My dad cried a lot too.
My mom butterflied a lamb, stuffed it with rosemary and garlic and invited people over for dinner.

The headmaster made me write a formal apology note to Dittmar promising never to disrupt his class again. During CAP Workshop, my Noel radar was in such a massive frenzy, I felt like I was going to have a panic attack every time I went—but I managed not to by taking off my glasses and letting the whole room blur, then singing retro metal songs in my head, ignoring everything Dittmar or anyone else said.

> *We will*
> *We will*
> *ROCK YOU.*
> *(Clap!*
> *Dum dum*
> *Clap!)*[1]

I still knew where he was, and my heart bounded every time he spoke, but Noel was just a soft outline of himself, not real Noel with his mouth in a thin line, making jokes with hateful, hateful Ariel Olivieri. I didn't feel guilt over his knee, which was still heavily wrapped, or guilt over wakeboarding with Gideon. At least, I didn't feel those things until I put my glasses back on and stopped singing in my head.

Mom brought an *entire dead piglet home* and dismembered it. She ground bits of it up to make sausage and

---

[1] "We Will Rock You." By Queen.

left its head sitting in the fridge while she researched ways of serving it.

I dared to suggest that this was a deeply inconsiderate and even cruel thing to do when one of the people you lived with had been a vegetarian for three years, and in response, Mom filled out Dittmar's parent questionnaire with the most obnoxious things she could think of to write and shoved it in my backpack. And as a performance artist, she writes obnoxious things *professionally.*

I found it at school during Calc. At first I thought, Ag, I have to turn this sheet of full-on madness in to Dittmar and he's going to think I'm even more insane than he already does. It's really going to hurt my chances in terms of getting any actual advice from him for my college applications—plus he'll show it to the other teachers and they'll all think I come from a completely certifiable family, and that's even without knowing that we found my dad this morning sitting in the shower stall wearing only his underwear and staring blankly at the tiles.

But then I thought: I don't have to give this paper to Dittmar.

I can tell him my parents keep not filling it out. Eventually, he'll forget about it.

I know better now than to throw any kind of incriminating document in the school trash can, so I ripped the questionnaire into tiny, tiny shreds and flushed it down the toilet.

"It was liberating," I told Doctor Z later. "Like I said,

I'm not letting this badness in my life. I'm flushing it down with all the poo."

The upside-down picture wasn't on her desk anymore. I was grateful because it was seriously distracting. Likewise, Doctor Z wasn't wearing an orange poncho or patchwork skirt or anything else so incredibly crafty and horrific that it detracted from my ability to have a therapeutic experience.

"My mother did this nasty thing," I went on, "but I didn't have to let it in. I mean, I have enough things in there tainting my brain. I don't need that."

"Good."

"I also didn't have to give the questionnaire to Dittmar. Even though he told us to turn it in. Sometimes, it's just better to ignore what you're supposed to do and do what's best for *you.*"

Doctor Z nodded. Then she asked: "What else do you think is tainting your brain?"

"Oh," I said. "Just my dad's depression, missing my dead grandma, our carnivorous household, Meghan always off with Finn, Nora always off with Kim and Cricket, Hutch in Paris, total isolation, mental illness, people who are cruel to animals, the question of whether to grow out my bangs, college applications, guilt over Noel, guilt over Gideon, major heartbreak and self-loathing. Nothing out of the ordinary."

"Well," Doctor Z said, crossing her legs, "can you flush any of *that?*"

"How could I flush it?"

"You tell me."

"These are not the kinds of things you can flush."

"Why not?"

"They're not pieces of paper. They're situations."

"What if you put them down on pieces of paper?"

"You're not serious."

"Sure. That can be a very therapeutic thing to do. You write out a problem that is bothering you, and then you flush it. Or burn it. Destroy it in some way as a gesture of setting yourself free."

"Yeah, but I can write my heartbreak down on paper six thousand times and flush it just as many. I'm still going to be heartbroken when I wake up in the morning. I'm still going to feel awful when I see Noel at school."

"Are you?"

"Yes."

"How do you know?"

"I just do."

"How do you know until you try?"

"You're serious."

"This week. Consider writing something that's bothering you on a piece of paper and flushing it," said Doctor Z. "It can be a small thing, if you want. It doesn't have to be your heartbreak, if you're wedded to that."

"I am *not* wedded to my heartbreak," I said. "I hate my heartbreak. I hate it." I was almost crying. "I am just *heartbroken*," I said. "There's nothing I can do about it."

"Really?" she said. "Really?"

●

After swim practice on Thursday I was in the B&O, reading *The Yellow Wallpaper* for Women Writers and cursing Mr. Wallace for insisting we both start and finish it over the weekend,[2] when Nora came in, her face swollen and pink. It was Finn's day off, so he and Meghan were somewhere else, doing couple things.

"Can I sit with you?" Nora asked.

We hadn't hung out since school started. She was friendly, and we chatted in the halls if we ran into each other, but most of the time she was in Kim and Cricket land.

"Knock yourself out," I told her. "You okay?"

---

[2] *The Yellow Wallpaper:* An 1899 novella by Charlotte Perkins Gilman about this lady whose doctor husband confines her to an attic room as a rest cure for her mental illness. She's not supposed to do *anything:* not read, not write, not play games, not have visitors, nothing. Wallace says this was the nineteenth-century idea of how to treat mental illness, or even just how to deal with difficult women. Lock them up and keep them quiet until they're ready to act the way society wants them to. Like a giant time-out. Naturally, the heroine of the story goes more and more insane because of this treatment that's supposedly going to make her better. By the end she thinks the wallpaper in her room is full of trapped women, and she has to strip it from the walls. She never leaves that room again. She just becomes a madman. So, yeah. It is supremely excellent that I don't live in 1899. First of all, I'd be married already (ag), and second of all, my husband would completely be locking me in the attic.

Nora sniffed and shook her head. "Not really."

"What happened? Something with Happy?"

"No, Happy's fine." She'd been arranging her tall frame on the chair across from me, digging around in her book bag, unwinding a cotton scarf she had around her neck. Now she looked at me and chewed on her thumbnail.

"What, then? Did I do something?" I asked.

"No."

"Is it about Noel?"

"Roo, please, can you stop asking and just let me tell you?"

My skin felt hot and I nodded silently.

"Kim, Cricket and I were on a three-way call just like an hour ago," she said. "Kim set it up so we could all talk about yearbook stuff while she had to be home supervising the gardener. I was talking to them on my cell from the photo lab where I was printing. I don't know where Cricket was, but anyway. We finished the yearbook stuff and I hung up and put the phone down without really looking at it, because I had a picture in the fixer and I realized it had been in there kinda long."

She stood up and ordered a black coffee from the guy at the counter. Like she didn't want to go on with the story. But black coffee doesn't take long to serve, and pretty soon Nora was back sitting across from me.

"So like ten minutes later I went to use the phone again and it had never hung up. I put it to my ear and Kim and Cricket were still talking." Nora wiped her eyes. "I know it's a bad thing to do, but I listened, and it didn't take long to figure out they were talking about me."

"Ag."

"Cricket was saying she was sick of hearing about Happy Happy Happy all the time, and Kim was saying I was just so controlling about yearbook, which is really unfair because I'm the editor, I'm supposed to be the boss of it, and she didn't have to be on it if she didn't want to."

"What did you do?"

"Cricket said I was no fun anymore and did I have to wear a stupid jog bra all the time, there was something about the jog bras that just really annoyed her and she couldn't stand to look at my uniboob one more day."

It was true. Nora did have the uniboob. But in her defense, she has these really ginormous hooters, and she's kind of self-conscious about them, so she squashes them down with the jog bra. Summer after freshman year, back when all four of us were friends, Kim and I had written an entry in our group notebook on "The Care and Ownership of Boobs"[3] that was in part intended to alert Nora to the uniboob issue that was going on. In fact, Kim and I had had a long discussion over whether to explicitly include information on the

---

[3] Joint notebook: Entitled *The Boy Book: A Study of Habits and Behaviors, Plus Techniques for Taming Them.*

uniboob problem, but we had eventually decided to leave it off because we were too scared of hurting Nora's feelings. We had hoped she would just read the instructions on the care and ownership and reexamine her own boob-related practices.

But she never did.

"Uniboob?" I said innocently. "What uniboob?"

"I don't know. I mean, how can she be mad at my *boobs*?" Nora wailed. "They never did anything to her."

"Your boobs are fantastic," I told her. Which was true. It was just her bras that were bad. "Maybe they stole attention from her. Maybe she's jealous of the way all the guys look at your chestal profile."

"Ugh." Nora grimaced. "Only guys like Neanderthal Darcy. Not quality guys."

"Maybe Cricket's in love with Neanderthal Darcy," I said. "Did you ever think of that?"

"I still haven't told you the worst part."

"Tell me."

Nora sipped her coffee and shook her head. "First, before I do: Roo, I want to say sorry."

"What for?"

"For not talking to you over the whole Noel business. For letting a guy come between us. For just—we've been friends a really long time and I should have acted different. When I was mad at you, I should have talked it out."

"Thanks," I said. It was good to hear her apologize, and I'd really never thought she would. But it did not escape my notice that she was saying all of this to me now, when not only did she have Happy but I had lost Noel. It's a lot easier to stop being jealous and mad when the girl who supposedly stole your guy is a heartbroken puddle of angst and everyone knows it.

"Yeah, well." Nora shook her head. "I feel like a third wheel with Cricket and Kim all the time. At lunch, at yearbook, out for coffee. It's like the two of them have something together that I don't have, like it doesn't matter whether I'm there or not, most of the time."

"Really?"

"My mom says three is just a difficult number," Nora went on, "but when I hung out with you and Meghan I never felt like a third wheel, ever. I just felt like we were all three friends. Like it was natural."

"It was," I said.

"Anyway, the thing I haven't told you yet is that Cricket said to Kim they should decide on a code word to use with each other when they want to get rid of me."

"A what?"

"Like, she said they should still be friends with me, but they didn't want me hanging around with them all the time. So whenever they wanted to ditch me, they'd say 'jog bra.'"

"And Kim agreed?"

Nora nodded. "She talked about how she didn't want to hurt my feelings but yeah, she was sick of me too. So if, like, they wanted to go to Top Pot Doughnuts after school—"

"Is that where they go now?" I said. Because neither

of them had set foot in the B&O since the debacles of sophomore year.

"Yeah. Anyway, if they wanted to go *without me,* because apparently I'm too controlling and boring and obsessed with my boyfriend, and my boobs are just so annoying Cricket wants to scream, then one would say something like, 'At crew practice my jog bra was cutting into my side in the worst way.' Then the other would know that they should both make excuses and leave me behind."

"You're kidding."

"No."

"Ag."

Nora reached over, picked up my fork and helped herself to a bite of my chocolate cheesecake. Just the way she used to. Before all the badness happened.

"What did you do?" I asked.

"Nothing. I started crying so I had to hang up the phone in case they heard me. Then I came to find you."

"We should make a code word for what complete wenches they are," I said.

"Like what?" Nora sniffed.

"Like *mushrooms.* I hate mushrooms."

"I like mushrooms."

"Okay, then what about *soybeans?*"

"Ugh."

"We can see them in the refectory and say things like, 'Oh, you know what really makes me ill? Soybeans!' And no one will know what we're talking about."

Nora kind of started laughing but then her face crumpled and she was crying. "I can't believe this happened," she said. "They've been my friends since forever."

"Mine too," I said. "Or were."

"How am I ever going to show my face at Tate again?" sobbed Nora. "Am I supposed to just go there and act like everything's okay, and smile at them and even sit with them, pretending like we're friends when I know they want to get rid of me? Or am I supposed to stop hanging around them, since they don't want me anyway, and act like I just happened to have other people to be with?"

"I don't know."

"Or am I supposed to be mad at them and not speak to them?" Nora wept. "I don't know how to even go to school in the morning."

Of course, this was exactly how I had felt ever since the debacles. Every day, I was walking into a hotbed of hostility and potential cruelty. But I didn't say that to Nora. What I said was: "I want to try something. Will you come in the bathroom with me?"

The B&O Espresso bathroom is painted dark purple and is not even big enough for one person. If you're in there on the toilet, you could completely wash your hands at the same time, without ever getting up. (Not that you would.)

I brought a marker, and Nora and I squeezed ourselves in there together. She is five eleven, so my face was practically in her uniboob, but I just went with it. I pulled off a long piece of toilet paper and wrote, in large letters: *The Wenchery of Cricket and Kim.* Then I gave it to Nora.

She took it and looked down at me. "What do you want me to do with this?"

"We're flushing it down with the poo," I told her.

"What?"

"The wenchery of Cricket! Down with the poo."

"Do you have to say *poo*?" Nora asked. "You could just say flush it down. You don't have to mention poo. There's no poo in there right now anyhow."

She was right. "We're flushing it," I told her. "Because we don't want it to have power over us. Because we don't want to be trapped in the yellow wall-paper."

"What's flushing it gonna do?"

"I have no idea," I admitted. "But my shrink wants me to do it. It's good for the mental health."

"But the wenchery is my problem," said Nora, waving her toilet paper sign. "Not yours."

Of course the wenchery of Cricket and Kim was a problem for me as well, but she was right. It wasn't looming large in comparison with my enormous freaking host of other problems. "Doctor Z wants me to flush my broken heart," I said. "But I don't think I can."

"Can you flush the Boneheadedness of Noel?" Nora asked. Which, given that she'd once crushed on him, was really a very nice thing to say.

I shook my head. "The problem isn't *his* bonehead-edness. The problem is that I'm deranged. Everything would have been okay if I wasn't such a mental patient."

"Okay. Seriously. *That's* what you have to flush," said Nora.

"What?" I didn't know what she was talking about.

"Come on, Roo," Nora was pulling a sheet of toilet paper off the roll. She grabbed my pen.

"What are you writing?" I tried to peek over her tall shoulder.

"Shush. You're going to thank me."

Someone knocked on the door of the B&O bathroom. "In a minute!" Nora yelled. "We're doing therapy homework!"

"Yes!" I called. "It's more important than urination!"

Nora handed me the toilet paper. In enormous letters she had written: *Self-loathing*.

"No, no, no," I said. "I can't give that up. Who would I be without my self-loathing?" I was being sarcastic, but Nora looked at me seriously.

"You could let it go, Roo. You're always saying awful stuff about yourself. Like you just called yourself a mental patient."

"But I am a mental patient."

"You make it sound like you're locked up in the asylum."

"Well," I joked, "it's only a matter of time."

Nora made an exasperated sound. "That's what I'm talking about."

"Okay, but it's not fair. You're getting to flush the badness of other people, but I have to flush the badness of myself."

The knock sounded again on the door of the bathroom. "Just a minute!" called Nora. "Roo. We have to flush now."

"Fine," I said. "We rip them up first."

Nora and I ripped our toilet paper signs into tiny shreds and dropped them into the paint-splattered toilet.

We flushed.

"Good riddance!" I yelled as the paper swirled down.

Then we opened the door to the bathroom and tumbled out of it, laughing hysterically.

●

Bonsoir, Hutch,

Comment va Paris? I have a mental image of you wearing your fanny pack and a beret, holding a baguette and playing bread air-guitar on the top deck of the Eiffel Tower.

But I know that can't be how you spend an average day.

Just on Saturdays, right?

Ruby,

The pastry of France kicks the ass of the pastry of America. It kicks it so hard the pastry of America hobbles to the curb whimpering, then scuttles down the street never to be seen again. That is how good the pastry is here.

Maybe you should come out at Thanksgiving break.

Or not. Whatever.

You probably have plans.

Hutch

Hutch,

No money, no Paris. That is the scenario here.

But I am glad you asked.

I would really like to see your bread air-guitar.

12.

Secrets of the Panda Bear!

Nora sits on the steps outside the Tate Prep gymnasium. She's dressed in shorts for basketball practice and looks all legs and uniboob under a tank top. Hair in a ponytail. She digs her camera out of her backpack and snaps a picture of Ruby behind the video camera.

>Nora: *There. You look like a real filmmaker.*
>Roo: *(behind the camera) Thank you.*
>Nora: *Meghan said you were going to ask me the definition of love. So I prepared an answer.*
>Roo: *That's what I asked her.*
>Nora: *Did you change?*
>Roo: *Now talk of love makes me feel desperate. I'm going to ask you about popularity.*
>Nora: *I'm not in love with Happy.*

Roo: You're not?

Nora: No. I mean, maybe I could be. But not yet. And
sometimes there are things he does that make me
think: I couldn't ever.

Roo: What?

Nora: Twice we've gone to parties and he's gotten really
wasted. I had to get the keys and drive us home. I
don't think I'm going to fall in love with someone
who gets drunk like that.

Roo: Couldn't you get him to stop?

Nora: Maybe I'll say something. But then would I fall in
love with him if he stopped? I don't know.

Roo: If he changed for you?

Nora: If he changed for me that would be nice. I guess.
But he'd still be the same person under the change.
The person who wants to get wasted. Who didn't
think anything about it until his girlfriend said
something.

Roo: Is that the answer you prepared?

Nora: (blushing) No. I was going to say, Love is when
you have a really amazing piece of cake, and it's the
very last piece, but you let him have it.

Roo: Nora.

Nora: What?

Roo: That's completely warped.

Nora: It's a metaphor. You like metaphors. Did I tell you
my brother's coming to town tonight for the weekend?
He gets in around five.

Roo: I have to turn this camera off.

Nora: He's always asking about you. Go out with him.
Roo: I can't find the right button.
Nora: I bet you'd have fun.
(darkness)

Gideon Van Deusen called me up that night. It was Halloween.

Every year, my parents go to this huge costume party Mom's friend Juana throws in some dance studio she's connected with. Lots of people in the Seattle arts community go, and my mother always wants to stand out.

This year, she had made go-together costumes: a light socket (her) and a plug (him). Dad stood in the middle of our living room wearing black leggings and a black thermal, his pelvis encased in a white cardboard box with two giant prongs sticking out like insane metal penises.

I was dressed as a bobby-soxer, wearing a vintage fifties dress I already owned but never wore, and saddle shoes I found for four dollars at the Salvation Army. I had curled my hair with Meghan's curling iron earlier that day and had my bangs pulled off my face with a totally retro hair band. I was planning to go to a soccer muffin party with Meghan, Finn and Nora, but I wasn't really looking forward to it. I'm not that interested in muffins, and seeing them dressed as Wolverine and Jack Sparrow doesn't make them any more attractive.

Anyway, Polka-dot trotted in from the bedroom. He eyed Dad's crotch prongs for only a moment before deciding they were chew toys and clamping his jaws around one of them. "No, Polka! Bad doggie!" Dad cried, swatting at the dog's nose and trying to move away from the drooling mouth.

The dog held fast.

"Ruby, get him off me!"

It was really not my idea of a pleasant evening to go sticking my hands in my father's pelvic region. I looked severely at the dog. "Polka. Drop it!"

Polka-dot shook his enormous head side to side, the way he did when he had a good stick in his mouth and wasn't no how going to drop it. Dad was practically hyperventilating, yelling, "Elaine, Polka's got my prongs!" but Mom was in the bedroom ignoring him, so I grabbed one of Polka's ears to stabilize his head and then pressed on the sides of his jaw to get him to loosen his grip on the prong.

Finally he opened his slavering mouth and I dragged him outside by the collar and clipped him to his chain.

Phew.

Inside, Dad was trying to sit down on the couch to rest after his trauma. However, his butt was encased in cardboard so he couldn't. The prong the dog had chewed was sagging, mangled and wet.

"Elaine, I told you this costume was a bad idea," Dad called.

Mom came in from the bedroom wearing a cardboard box with two light sockets on it. Her hair was gelled up to look like she'd been electrocuted. "Don't be so negative, Kevin," she said. "You're negative all the time now. You have to get over yourself."

"Polka ate my prong," Dad said. "I can't even sit down."

"You look hot," Mom said. "The prongs are very sexy."

"The left one is ruined."

"We can fix it with duct tape."

"I don't know how I'm supposed to drive when I can't even sit."

"You're not driving. We're taking public transportation."

"I still can't sit."

"You can stand on the bus." Mom stroked her electric-shock hair. "What do you think? Adds to the effect, right?"

"Can we please just wear the silly hats instead?" Dad begged.

"If you don't like being the plug you can be the outlets," Mom said, making as if to take off her box.

"I am not being the outlets."

"Why not?"

"I'm just not."

"You shouldn't be scared of your feminine side, Kevin. Everyone has one," said Mom glibly. "I'd be glad to wear the prongs."

"Mom!" I cried. "Leave him alone! The dog just tried to eat his pelvis."

She turned on me. "You stay out of this, Ruby. I already know you're on your father's side; you're *always* on your father's side."

"You don't have to be such a wench to him."

"You know what?" said Mom angrily. "I don't have to stand for this. Not your smart mouth or your father's apathy. I'm going on vacation. Without either of you. Starting tomorrow morning."

"What?" Dad look shocked.

"Juana asked me yesterday if I wanted to drive down to the Oregon coast with her women's empowerment group, and I told her no, because I felt guilty leaving you when you're still moping about Suzette's death."

"Don't miss it on my account," Dad said bitterly.

"And Ruby. Ruby's being a drama queen about this thing with Noel what'shisname. The two of you are driving me crazy with all your negativity and self-involvement," she said. "So you know what? I don't feel guilty anymore. I don't need to work so hard stuffing sausages and making Halloween costumes when no one appreciates anything I do. I can go to Oregon and sit in a hot spring!"

"I did appreciate the sausages," said my dad. "I made a point of telling you I liked them."

"Roo didn't."

"I'm a vegetarian!" I yelled.

"I'll be leaving tomorrow morning," said my mother. "It will be a relief to get away from both of you."

She stomped into the bedroom and emerged with

her purse, furiously putting lipstick on. Then she slammed the front door and walked—awkwardly in her costume—into the fading light.

When she was out of sight, Dad took off his cardboard box, let Polka back in the house and gave him the costume. Polka chewed on it, thumping his tail heavily on the carpet.

Dad lay facedown on the floor beside the dining table and announced he was just going to rest there for a minute.

"Aren't you going to go after Mom?"

"I gave the prongs to the dog," he said. "There's no way I can be forgiven unless I have prongs."

"Are you going to let her go on vacation without us?" I said. "Is she really going to leave?"

"I don't know," Dad said, turning his head to rest the alternate cheek on the carpet. "Your mother pretty much does what she wants to do."

"Are you depressed?" I asked, standing over him. It was a stupid question. Of course he was depressed. He was the king of being depressed.

"I'm just so tired."

"Dad! You have to do something. She's leaving us."

"Will you answer the phone?"

"What?"

"The phone."

Oh. It was ringing. I picked it up, thinking it would be Mom calling from her cell, but instead it was Gideon. "Hey, wakeboarder," he said.

"Hey, wakeboarder yourself."

"Happy Halloween."

"Same to you."

"What are you doing right now?"

"Trying to peel my dad off the floor."

"Ha-ha," said Gideon. "You want to come to a party with me?"

"I'm supposed to go to this soccer party with Nora."

"She told me you'd rather do something else."

"She did?"

"She said something about muffins."

I laughed. "Yeah. Is yours a costume party?"

"Of course."

"What are you being?"

"A bad surgeon. But I need to get fake blood. I forgot to get fake blood."

"Use ketchup."

"Good idea. I'm going to squirt myself with ketchup and pick you up in half an hour."

"I'm going out, Dad," I said when I hung up. "Are you going to be okay?"

He didn't answer. He was asleep.

Gideon kissed me before we even got to the party. I wasn't ready. As we got into his hybrid, he leaned over and very simply put his lips on mine–not like he was lunging at me or anything, just impulsive and sweet.

He smelled like ketchup. He was wearing a white

doctor's coat and a stethoscope. There was a rubber severed hand sticking out of his pocket.

We kissed for a minute and then he said: "I've been wanting to do that for like, years."

"I was way too young for you," I said.

"You're too young for me now," he said. "But you're older than you were."

"Maybe it's *you* who's too old for *me*," I told him.

"Maybe we should be quiet and kiss a little more," he said, leaning in.

The thing about kissing Gideon was he was a lot more experienced than any other guy I'd kissed. I mean, there was no way he was still a virgin. He had traveled around the world for a year and then started at Evergreen College, which was full of people who still lived by the "make love, not war" slogans of the sixties. In other words, Gideon's kissing was the kissing of a guy who knows exactly what this kind of thing can lead to, and who has long since been done with two-hour make-out sessions where everyone keeps their clothes on. The people he was used to kissing obviously had full and intimate knowledge of the nether regions and what to do if one encountered them.

It was a little slobbery for my taste, to be honest.

"You have to put the severed hand in the back," I said after a minute or two. "It's freaking me out."

He threw it over his shoulder to the backseat, where it landed with a creepy squish. "I'll kiss you some more later," he said. "We're late for the party." He turned the key in the ignition.

"I've never kissed anyone who talked so much about kissing," I told him.

Gideon laughed. "I like to be direct."

"Okay," I said. "But I warn you, I like to be evasive, inscrutable and generally send mixed messages."

"I doubt it."

"Human interaction is not my strong point," I told him.

"Not seriously."

"Seriously," I said. Thinking: There is so much about me he doesn't know.

Gideon put his hand on my leg. "What's your strong point, then?" he asked.

"Goats," I told him. "I am excellent with goats."

The party was a college party.

I was out with a college guy, I suppose I should have known I was going to a college party, but I was so intent on getting away from Dad and his misery that I hadn't really thought about where Gideon was taking me. It turned out to be a the apartment of this guy Ted Hsaio (pronounced Shaw) who'd been in Gideon's year at Tate and was now a junior at the University of Washington.

Hsaio lived just off the Ave in the U District, in a studio apartment. As we walked down the hall, I could hear the roar of voices coming from his place, and when Gideon opened the door we saw a wall of people, all in costume, jammed up against each other and smoking, plastic cups of beer clutched in their hands. "Van Deusen!" Hsaio yelled when he saw Gideon. They fake-sparred, the way guys do when they don't want to hug, and finally Gideon threw his bloody rubber hand at Hsaio. Hsaio was dressed as a fisherman in waders and a hat. He carried a fishing pole and had several plastic fish sticking out of his pockets. "Who's your new girl?" he yelled at Gideon over the din.

"What?" Gideon yelled back in Hsaio's ear.

"Who's your girl?" said Hsaio, even louder.

"This is Ruby."

I waved.

"Cradle robbing?" Hsaio asked Gideon.

"Shut up."

"Dude, we'd all do it if we could."

"Same as ever, huh, Hsaio?"

"Why change what's working?" Hsaio laughed.

Gideon grabbed my hand and pulled me to the tiny kitchen, where a cadaver and two lady pirates were filling cups from a keg and mixing some kind of drink called a kamikaze. Two girls in slut costumes were sitting on the countertops and a guy in a gorilla suit leaned against the fridge. It smelled of sweat and booze.

Gideon handed me a cup of beer, which I didn't want, and then grabbed a guy dressed as Jackie Onassis into a bear hug. "DuBoise!" he cried. "What the hell are you doing here?"

DuBoise.

DuBoise? I sloshed half my beer down my dress.

"Van Deusen," the Jackie O said. He was wearing a pillbox hat and a black bouffant wig with a sweet purple vintage suit and heels.

Noel's brother, Claude.

"Who knew you were home?" Gideon said.

"Came back last week."

"Isn't it the middle of the term?"

Claude nodded. His eye makeup was running and his lipstick smudged down his chin. "New York was . . ." He shook his head. "I came back for a while is all."

Claude had been in Gideon's class at Tate. That was how come I recognized him, even though he'd never been home to Seattle in all the time I'd been friends with Noel.

In high school, Claude had been golden. He'd gone out with several girls. He'd been a soccer player and a rower, a model of Young American Manhood. I knew from Noel that when Claude realized he was gay, freshman year at NYU, some of his old high school friends had been jerks about it—which was why he didn't usually come home in the summers.

Now here he was, back in town and wearing full drag at a party full of Future Doctors of America and other kinds of prepsters from his past. As if to say, Up yours if you don't like me. This is who I am.

Which was cool. I mean, Claude clearly wasn't worried about becoming a roly-poly. He didn't care what people thought anymore. He was out and proud.

He wouldn't recognize me, I thought. Though he probably knew my name from Noel. I'd been a freshman when he, Gideon and Hsaio were seniors.

Part of me wanted to meet Claude, talk to him, find out anything I could about Noel—whom I saw at school but never spoke to anymore.

The other part wanted to run, for fear Claude would tell Noel he saw me out with Gideon.

That part won.

I pressed out of the kitchen into the main room of the apartment and squeezed through a mass of sweaty, makeup-covered bodies to a spot near an open window. I leaned my back against it, feeling the cool breeze trickle into the hot room.

Everyone was tipsy, and many people had taken off bits of their costumes in the heat. Hats and bunny ears and capes were piled on an armchair. Everyone was at least three years older than I was and they all knew each other. The guys had broad shoulders and stubble on their faces. A few people were familiar from Tate, years ago, but most were probably Hsaio's U Dub friends. It seemed—just way more *advanced* than high school parties. Everyone was smoking; no one had a curfew.

I was standing there, trying to look relaxed and as if I went to college parties every day and oh, yeah, I'm just leaning on this windowsill here because it's so completely comfortable, I always do this at parties—when I saw Noel. He was dressed as Johnny Rotten, which I could tell because he had a Sex Pistols[1] poster in his room. His blond hair was dyed electric orange and spiked up with even more than his usual amount of gel. He had on tight black cigarette jeans, a heavy black leather jacket, combat boots and an old plaid flannel shirt. He wore a fake earring in one ear and had a mole drawn on the left side of his cheek.

And he was talking to a girl. A pretty, pretty, pretty girl. Taller than me, slim, with short dark hair and makeup that said: Sexy Vampire. A tight black T-shirt, a fringed skirt and high red heels.

She was leaning in to talk to Noel.

He was leaning in to talk to her.

Ag. Ag. Ag.

I thought:

1. If Noel sees me here with Gideon, he'll think for sure I cheated on him back in September and we'll never get back together. I have to hide or leave—or something.

2. On the other hand, he might have a surge of jealousy and chase after me down the hallway as I'm leaving Hsiao's. He'll punch Gideon in the face just for taking me out to a party and declare his love. Then we can live happily ever after.

3. Then again, what makes me think we could *ever* get back together? Noel obviously doesn't love me anymore. He doesn't even speak to me.

---

[1] The Sex Pistols: A British retro punk band known for the song "Anarchy in the UK."

4. He is probably going out with this sexy college vampire now. I should just forget about him.
5. On the other hand, if he sees me standing alone by the window, he might witness my deep and tragic loneliness and remember how much he loves me. Maybe I look melancholy and alluring.
6. Although more likely, he'll see me alone and think I look pathetic and repulsive.
7. I should go talk to him.
8. No. I shouldn't.

Noel encounters me nearly every day at school and we never say anything more than hello in the most awkward way possible. Why would it be any different here?

9. There isn't really anything I can do at a Halloween party to make him love me again! Talking to him is bound to end in angst and misery. I should stay here.
10. No. I should run away.

As I was dithering and trying to look attractive and wondering whether Gideon would come in looking for me, Noel leaned down and kissed the sexy college vampire girl.

On the lips.

She kissed him back and I felt sick, my heart thrashing, like I was getting a panic attack standing here in Hsaio's living room. Suddenly the most important thing was to get out of that hot, smoky room and breathe. I didn't care who saw me or didn't see me or anything, I just wanted out.

I pushed my way through the crowd and into the kitchen. Gideon was there, and I grabbed him by the arm. "I'm really, really sorry, but can we leave? *I* need to leave, at least. I can take a bus if you can't drive me."

"I'll drive you." He raised his eyebrows. "You okay?"

"Not really. Can we just go? You can come back later if you want."

Without waiting for him, I pushed out the door and down the hall and took the stairs down to the building lobby.

Don't panic, I told myself. You don't need to panic.

You're sad and jealous and embarrassed, but this is not the end of the world.

You're healthy. You're not having a heart attack.

There's enough air here for you to fill your lungs.

Just breathe, Ruby.

Breathe and remember you're okay.

I put a mint in my mouth and concentrated on the flavor. I breathed.

And breathed.

When Gideon arrived in the lobby I was able to smile at him. "Sorry to drag you out," I said. "My ex-boyfriend was there and I think I'm allergic to him."

Gideon laughed. "You said you weren't direct."

"Well, I'm direct about some things."

"I was kind of looking forward to mixed messages and—what did you say? Inscrutability."

He was so optimistic. That was the key to Gideon.

As if now that we'd been out together, we were going out together a whole lot more. Like he had stuff to look forward to, stuff to do with him and me.

"Sorry to disappoint you," I said.

"You'd have to work really, really hard to do that," he said, taking my hand.

And just like that, possibly because I'm psychotic, I wanted to kiss him again. He was so hot, in his doctor's coat with his thick dark eyebrows and his sweet ketchup smell and his ugly Birkenstocks on his feet. And I thought: Noel will never love me.

My mom is leaving us.

My dad is depressed.

All that badness, and yet here, standing in front of me, is something good.

Someone good.

Gideon Van Deusen. Shouldn't I be thankful for what life brings me instead of wanting what I can't have?

Yes, I should.

That must be the key to happiness, right?

And couldn't I—as Doctor Z was always implying— couldn't I *choose happiness*?

So it wasn't psychotic to want to kiss Gideon so soon after mooning over Noel. It was mentally stable and healthy!

As we stepped out onto the street, I reached up and put my hand on Gideon's neck. I drew his face down to mine. He wrapped his arms around me, and he was wonderfully tall, and when I put my hands on him, his waist was hard and athletic and he just seemed like a *man* and not a boy.

I thought: This is such a better idea than being with Noel.

And then I thought:

1. I wonder if Noel will walk out of the party and see me.
2. Don't think that, you boy-crazy lunatic. Just kiss Gideon and feel lucky.
3. Yeah, but what would happen if Noel did walk out of the party and see me?
4. Brain, shut up. Shut UP!

Noel didn't walk out of the party.

Gideon and I spent the rest of the evening strolling the Ave and looking at people in costume. Lots of college kids spilling out of bars and on their way to parties, girls in sexy nurse costumes, sexy cowgirl, sexy devil. We got smoothies from a stand, blackberry for me and strawberry-peach for him. We talked about movies, and Gideon's travels in Egypt.

I told him this stuff I heard at Woodland Park Zoo: how in China they've started breeding pandas to save them from extinction and now there are all these baby pandas in a care center. It's kind of like an orphanage, only they're not orphans. You can see videos of them on YouTube: a whole pile of baby bears crawling on each other and squinting out of half-opened eyes. "They're artificially inseminated, though, because pandas are pretty much uninterested in sex, especially when they live in zoos," I said. "In fact, a few years ago these zoologists made panda porno to get the young male pandas interested and explain to them what to do."

"What?"

"Other animals, you put a male and a female together and they figure it out—but apparently pandas really cannot get the hang of it without help. So they made dirty movies. It was the audio component that made the most difference, the scientists found. The panda heavy breathing. If they didn't have the audio on, the pandas just got bored."

Gideon laughed. I mean, it's funny. But I couldn't help thinking how Noel would have riffed on the whole panda thing. He would have on-the-spot made up silly rhymes about the pandas, or sketched some completely risqué panda on a paper napkin, or made up a business plan for renting X-rated videos out to various zoos to help endangered species, probably the only possible career path that would combine porno and ecology. Something.

Gideon asked me serious questions about pandas. Like, did I know how many there were left in the world? And did they eat anything besides bamboo?

I didn't know the answers. Because I love animals and learning stuff about them, but the truth is, I like amusing and strange animal stories much more than I like factoids about their everyday lives. I like gay egg-stealing penguins better than straight, socially responsible penguins, and I like porn-watching panda bears and piles of itty-bitty pandas in an orphanage better than just regular old pandas doing their thing in the wild.

But I didn't quite want to admit that to Gideon.

So I kissed him again and he seemed to forget about the questions he was asking.

13.

The Mysterious Disappearance of Kevin!

Gideon sits on a bench outside his dorm at Evergreen College. He's wearing a knit cap and a sleeveless parka over a chamois shirt. Birkenstocks and socks.

> Roo: (behind the camera) What's your definition of popularity?
>
> Gideon: Popularity? Nora said you were making a documentary about friendship and love.
>
> Roo: And popularity.
>
> Gideon: I haven't thought about that since maybe ninth grade.
>
> Roo: Really?
>
> Gideon: Really.
>
> Roo: Maybe that's because you're popular. You're so popular you've never had to think about it.

Gideon: *I don't think so.*

Roo: *Trust me. You were golden in high school.*

Gideon: *(ducking his head) I had friends.*

Roo: *Popular!*

Gideon: *Hardly.*

Roo: *If you had* ever *been unpopular, you would be concerned with it in one way or another.*

Gideon: *That seems warped.*

Roo: *I mean, even if you rejected the idea of popularity, you'd have at least thought about it.*

Gideon: *If you say so.*

Roo: *Here's a test: when was the last time you spent a Saturday night home alone?*

Gideon: *I don't know.*

Roo: *Exactly.*

Gideon: *But that's not because I'm popular. That's 'cause if I don't have something to do, I call someone up and go out.*

Roo: *But you have someone to call up.*

Gideon: *Yeah. Of course.*

Roo: *That's my point.*

When I returned home on Halloween, my mother was still out at Juana's party. Before I woke up the next morning, she was gone, presumably to Oregon with Juana.

She didn't leave a note and she didn't call.

Dad was still lying on the floor when I got up, and he

grunted at me when I told him Mom was gone, but didn't answer any of my questions.

For the next ten days I tried to forget about Noel and the sexy college vampire girl, forget about the disappearance of my mother (who didn't answer her cell) and forget that my father was eating nothing but Doritos, Cheese Nips, Cheez-Its, Cheetos and other bright orange cheese-flavored snack foods, sitting on the couch and watching bad television. He even slept there at night, drooling orange drool onto the front of the same sweatshirt he'd been wearing for days.

I pretended everything was normal and excellent. I shot videos for my college application film, did my schoolwork, baked cupcakes for Meghan's birthday and went out with Gideon.

He took me out to the movies a couple of nights, and to dinner. He was acting like a real live boyfriend right away. Calling me, showing up on time, holding my hand. He was very easy to be around, though I didn't let him in the house or tell him what was going on with my parents. Instead, I treated being with him like an escape from the realities of my life and the things in my heart.

Gideon almost always had a paperback book in his pocket, philosophy or history, in which he underlined enthusiastically and which he pulled out to read if he ever had to wait for anything. Like if I went to the bathroom at a restaurant, he'd be reading when I came back. He was also studying Spanish and he had this funny instructional CD in his car. He wanted to learn Spanish because he planned to travel to South America with this charity organization to build latrines and help with immunizations and stuff.

So he was basically an awesome human, and yet periodically I'd think: Is there something secretly wrong with him that he wants to go out with a high school girl? And a neurotic high school girl, at that?

Maybe he seems like a normal guy but he'll turn out to be an absolute psycho like Edward Norton in *Primal Fear*. Or Edward Norton in *Fight Club*. Or Edward Norton in *The Incredible Hulk*.

Then I'd remind myself that I'd flushed my self-loathing down with all the poo, and tell myself I was a smart and pretty person and there was no reason why a hot college guy who wanted to go out with me was automatically a secret lunatic.

Truthfully, the only thing I could find wrong with Gideon was that he wasn't the greatest kisser. He was slobbery and overly sex-tongue-y about it. And he smelled like patchouli, which isn't bad per se but reminded me of my boss at the Birkenstock store, which was a very unromantic association.

One Saturday he drove me up to Evergreen for the day to show me around the campus. It was lush and green and had bicycles parked all over and leaflets posted up about open-mike nights and art shows and bands. I had never been on a college campus besides the UW, which is right in the middle of Seattle, and that's so large and manicured and full of graduate-student future lawyers and stuff that it doesn't seem like *college* college.

"I don't think I realized until now that this time next year I'll not only be out of the Tate Universe, I'll be out of my parents' house," I told Doctor Z later that week. "I'll be living *alone*. In like, New York City or Philadelphia or Los Angeles."

"Uh-huh."

"I'll have to take care of myself."

She just looked at me.

"What?"

More looking.

"I'm pretty much taking care of myself right now, since Mom left. Is that what you're thinking?"

"It crossed my mind," she admitted.

"Well, I just bring home take-out pizza and eat cereal for breakfast. It's not like I've scrubbed the oven or anything."

She nodded.

"Although I did clean the bathroom yesterday," I admitted. "And I made Dad change his clothes and take a shower."

"How did that feel?" Doctor Z asked me.

I hate it when she says shrinky things like that.

"I am trying not to have feelings about it at all," I said. "And I'm succeeding pretty well."

"Are you getting support from your friends? From Nora or Meghan?"

I shook my head. "I haven't said anything."

"Why not?"

"I'm sick of being Neurotic Ruby whose life is always in a crisis. I'm sick of self-loathing and self-pity. So I'm flushing it down," I told her. "Crazy dad drooling Cheeto juice. Flush! Disappearing act by Mom. Flush! Dead Grandma. Flush! Noel with someone else. Flush! And then it's like magic: no feelings!"

Doctor Z leaned forward. "I didn't mean for you to pretend difficult situations don't exist," she said. "There are some things you can't flush."

Yeah, well.

"There's a difference between letting something go," Doctor Z continued, "releasing yourself of tension or a negative way of thinking—"

"You told me to flush and I flushed!" I protested.

"There's a difference between stopping an obsessive thought pattern," she said, "and denying your feelings or stuffing them down."

Ag again. "You want me to do Reginald," I said. "But I don't want to do Reginald. I want to flush it all down and have a lobotomy."

She smiled. "Those aren't the same thing," she said. "Flushing is setting yourself free of negativity, and the lobotomy is denial."

"Fine."

"Didn't you use that word *lobotomy* about Noel?" Doctor Z asked.

"Probably."

"Remind me what you said."

"He was acting like he'd had one. I told him that and he got mad."

Doctor Z nodded. "So what's the similarity between Noel's lobotomy and the lobotomy you want to have?"

I just didn't want to feel the things I felt. I wanted to go out with Gideon and dream about college and just ignore the badness so completely that it wouldn't affect me.

Oh.

Could that be what Noel was doing too?

Ignoring some badness so completely he was lobotomized?

"This isn't making me happy," he had said. "I came back from New York and I thought you would make me happy but I'm not happy."

"But is that really a girlfriend's job?" I asked Doctor Z, out of context. "To make someone happy who's unhappy to start with?"

She just went with my change of subject. "What do you think?"

I shifted in my seat. "I think maybe it's impossible to cheer people up when they're really sad. I think they just have to be sad and all you can do is hang out with them because you love them."

Doctor Z nodded.

"But then again," I said, "if they're drooling Cheeto drool out their mouths and watching daytime television for days and days on end, forgetting to shower, you may stop wanting to hang around them."

Doctor Z leaned forward. "Are we talking about Noel or your father?"

"I don't know," I answered. "I honestly don't know."

Dad wasn't there when I came home from therapy on the bus.

He didn't come back at dinnertime—not that there was dinner, really, but I did order pizza.

I got worried around ten o'clock and called his cell.

It rang on his desk. He didn't have it with him.

At one in the morning, when he still wasn't home, I called Mom's cell, but she didn't pick up. I hadn't talked to her in the ten days since she left, but I'd been too mad to call more than twice.

In the morning, I called her again. No answer.

So I called Meghan.

"You're calling early," she chirped.

"My dad's gone missing," I told her. "And he took the car."

"What?"

As soon as I heard the concern in her voice, it all spilled out. How Mom left in a huff for an extended vacation. Dad drooling on the couch and sleeping on the floor, depression over Grandma Suzette and more depression over Mom leaving.

"Why didn't you tell me?" Meghan said.

"You were busy with Finn," I said. "And I was trying to pretend it wasn't happening."

"I'm coming over," said Meghan.

When she saw the state of our houseboat, she cringed. Old pizza boxes, dog food spilled on the floor, empty cans of pop piled on top of the fridge. Kitchen sink stacked with dishes, garbage cans overflowing. "Denial isn't working for you, sweetie," she said. "I'm calling Nora and we're going to clean this place up."

"We have to find my dad first," I said. "He might be dead."

Meghan laughed. Until she realized I was serious. "Let's check his e-mail."

So we did. It was already downloaded and the program open on his computer. We didn't have to enter a password or anything.

He had been reading his mail, apparently, despite appearances to the contrary. Nearly every message was open, and a few had reply marks next to them.

"There are notes from your mom here," Meghan said.

"Really?" As far as I knew, Dad hadn't heard from her since Halloween.

"Yeah." Meghan opened the most recent one.

Kevin,

The coast is gorgeous.

Miss you.

I have an idea for a new show that Juana is helping me outline. It's been almost a year and a half since I've been onstage, and I think that's why I've been miserable.

You know I hate copyediting, and if I don't perform anymore, my whole life will be copyediting when Ruby goes off to college. Do you see?

The women's retreat has got me writing again.

Also, I bought a red negligee. I'll show it to you when I get back.

Love,

Elaine

"Ag," I said. "I did not need to read that last bit."

"Your parents are so cute together," Meghan said. "They're in love."

"They're insane and neglectful," I said.

"But in a cute way."

"What do you mean?"

"She's on the seashore. She's finding herself," said Meghan. "She needed a break from him, but now she misses him."

"At least they're not getting divorced," I said. "I thought they were probably getting divorced."

"They're not getting divorced if she wants to show him her red negligee."

I shook my head to get the bad image out. "We need to find my dad," I reminded Meghan.

"He's probably not dead," she said consolingly. "He'd stay alive for the negligee."

We looked at the e-mails again. Lots of questions about container gardening, a note from Hutch about working again when he returned in December, more container gardening. Then there was one from Greg, Dad's neurotic friend with the panic disorder, dated yesterday.

He said he'd sprained his ankle in the shower and was in the "slough of despond."

I called Greg, even though it was eight a.m. He picked up on the third ring.

"Hi. Um. Sorry to call so early. It's Ruby, Kevin's daughter."

"Hello, Ruby."

"Dad never came home last night and I'm wondering if maybe he came to visit you?"

"He's passed out on the couch," said Greg.

Meghan and I drove to Greg's place. We banged on the door for ten minutes before I heard Greg shuffling behind it. "Who's there?" he said. He's so messed up with the panic attacks he's afraid to open the door.

"It's Ruby!" I called.

Greg's voice was defensive. "I don't receive until after noon."

"I know you're up. I just talked to you on the phone," I told him.

Greg cracked the door, then walked back into the apartment without greeting us. Meghan and I followed him. He was limping.

There were stacks and stacks of old newspapers and magazines lining the walls, and huge windows filled with plants. The desk was buried under old food cartons and paper, but out of it surged a large computer monitor Greg used for writing software. In one corner was an enormous flat-screen TV. In another was a Habitrail filled with wood chips and gerbils.

"This is my friend Meghan," I told Greg.

He flinched but held out his hand to her.

Dad was asleep in his boxer shorts on Greg's hairy brown couch. Greg shook him awake.

"Hey, Ruby," Dad said, groggy.

"Are you okay?" I said. "What are you doing here?"

"I'm fine. It just got late, so I crashed." He sat up and pulled an afghan over his lap.

"You're really okay?"

"Yeah. Of course."

"Then I am so mad at you, Dad!" I yelled. "How could you not call? Or leave a note, or anything? I was all alone in the house! I couldn't reach Mom. I had no idea what had happened to you! I thought you jumped off a bridge!"

"I know, I know," he said.

"You don't know," I grouched. "You don't know I thought you jumped off a bridge. You don't know I called Mom."

He shook his head. "I would never jump off a bridge."

"How am I supposed to know that when you lie on the floor all the time drooling Cheeto juice like a complete madman?"

Dad smiled. "Wow, you paint a pretty picture."

"Seriously!"

Dad stood up and put on his pants, looking infuriatingly cheerful and not all that apologetic. "I know I was wrong not to call, Ruby," he said.

"Then why didn't you?"

"Three little words."

"What words?"

"Guitar. Hero. Metallica." Dad pointed at the Wii on the coffee table. "We stayed up till four in the morning."

"Let me make sure I understand," I said flatly. "I thought you were dead and you were having Dude Time playing Guitar Hero."

"He kicked my butt," Greg chirped. "But he made up for it by running out for Chinese and an Ace bandage. I messed my ankle up the other day," he explained.

"Doesn't he know he has a kid?" I barked at Greg. "Doesn't he know I've been worrying about him all night? What kind of father forgets to come home?"

"The game really cheered him up," Greg explained. "I bought it for him back in September, but I never had a chance to give it to him."

"I was processing a lot after my mom died," Dad said to Meghan by way of explanation. "I didn't return his calls."

"He's been depressed to the point of neglecting personal hygiene," I said to Greg.

Dad ran his fingers through his hair. "Yeah, I guess I was," he said. As if it were far in the past. As if he hadn't been lying on the floor *yesterday.* "Then Greg hurt his ankle, so, you know, I had to get up."

"Your wife leaving you isn't enough to get you up?" I said.

"She didn't leave me. She took a break to go to Oregon with Juana."

"That's leaving."

He shook his head. "That's marriage. It's complicated."

"She acted like she was leaving. She hasn't called."

"Well, she left in a huff. But you know your mother. She loves to get into a huff over things."

That was true.

"I know it's hard to understand," Dad continued patronizingly, "but Mom felt helpless and disempowered."

"You know Elaine hates being disempowered," laughed Greg.

My dad continued: "She was fighting with you all the time, fighting with me; the stress was too much for her, so she took a break. I thought you understood that."

"No."

"You acted so chipper, going out with your new boyfriend and everything. I thought for once I didn't have to worry about you."

"It's called denial, Dad!" I yelled. "It's not exactly healthy!"

Dad stood up. "Greg," he said. "I'm sorry to bring an argument into your place. It's not good repayment for the rockin' evening of Metallica."

"That's all right," said Greg.

"Meghan and I have to get to school," I said. "Dad,

will you be home for dinner tonight? I'm ordering it at seven and you're in charge of dessert."

"Yes, Ruby," he said resignedly. "I'll be home."

Getting behind the wheel of her Jeep, Meghan sighed. "That poor Greg," she said. "He really never leaves the house?"

"That's totally what I'll be like if I can't head-shrink myself into some kind of mental stability," I said.

"A shut-in with a Habitrail?" Meghan crinkled her nose. "I don't think so."

"Oh, just you wait. I'll have, like Great Danes and pygmy goats and maybe even a baby panda living with me. That's what panic does to people if the attacks get bad enough."

"You would never have a paisley bathrobe, though."

"Seriously. Sometimes I don't want to go places because I'm scared I'll panic."

"Like where?"

"Like school. Like CAP Workshop."

"But you go to school."

"Yeah, and I go to the stupid workshop, but my point is: I almost don't. I can completely see how Greg got to be shut in like he is. I look at him and see my future sometimes."

"Roo."

"What? I'm being honest."

"When was the last time you had a panic thing?"

Meghan asked. "'Cause I haven't seen or heard you talk about one since, like, the start of the summer."

"I have them—" I was about to say I had them all the time. But she was right.

I hadn't had one.

Not when Noel and I fought.

Not when he fell down the stairs.

Not when he ignored me at school.

Or kissed that girl.

Not when Dad lay on the floor. And Mom left.

I had not panicked.

Sometimes I had to sing retro metal in my head and breathe deep, or take off my glasses and be semi-blind, or cut class and take a shower—but I hadn't had a panic thing in a very long time.

14.

Shocking Disclosure in the Zoological Gardens!

Dear Robespierre,

Happy Thanksgiving.

I wonder if goats feel neurotic on holidays, like people do. When I was little, Thanksgiving and Christmas were just parties and pretty dresses and desserts. Then last year, I realized what a drunk Uncle Hanson is, and how stressed Dad and Grandma Suzette were. Suddenly, it wasn't a party. It was an ordeal.

This year, I'm worried Dad will melt down again and start talking about his dead mother, just when he's started to get up in the mornings and work on his newsletter. Also Uncle Hanson will be there and no Grandma Suzette to make jokes and encourage him to act normal. Plus Mom is making a turducken[1], and there's nothing like a big

---

[1] A turducken is a boned chicken stuffed into a boned duck stuffed into a partly boned turkey, all layered in with stuffing and—well, it's a triple-crown meat extravaganza, that's all you need to know.

meat-eating holiday to make her mad that I don't eat what she cooks. So it'll be a miracle if we make it through Thanksgiving without a descent into seriously bad family dynamics.

Wish me luck.

Love,

Ruby Oliver

—written on zoo stationery with a ballpoint pen and folded into a small rectangle.

My mother came home with gifts. A T-shirt for my dad that said DOG IS MY COPILOT and a vintage dress for me.

It fit, too.

I was angry at her for leaving, but I also had to admit that it had been good to have her gone. Good for me and Dad to just take care of ourselves, even if we did it badly. Good for us to hang around together without her giant personality heaving itself between us. She came back full of ideas for the new show she wanted to do, plans for the holiday season, stories about her adventures with Juana and the women's empowerment group. She was less on the attack, somehow.

I worked at the zoo the weekend before Thanksgiving, mucking out stalls in the Family Farm area early on Sunday morning. When I finished that, I went to help Lewis the plant guy trim some hedges. Perversely, though I complain about helping Dad in the greenhouse, I like trimming hedges. The clippers are really big. I feel tough hacking stray bits of greenery into submission.

I was chopping away and not thinking about anything when suddenly two sets of round arms wrapped themselves around my waist: Sydonie and Marie. "We're at the zoo! We saw the elephant already," cried Marie.

"Claude didn't know where the bathrooms were," said Sydonie. "I had to show him."

"Is Noel with you?" I asked, nervous.

"No, Claude! Didn't you hear me? Of course *Noelie* knows where the bathrooms are."

I looked up and there was Claude, looking like Noel, only with dark hair and broad shoulders. Same delicate profile, same pale eyes. He was dressed in blue striped pants and a red cashmere sweater–vaguely nautical and a touch flamboyant. "They know you, apparently," he said.

"Um. Yes."

"It's Ruby!" shouted Marie.

"Noelie's girlfriend!" shouted Sydonie.

Claude's eyes widened. "You're Ruby?"

I felt like I must be a disappointment. I was wearing an ugly zoo uniform and no makeup.

"I'm not Noel's girlfriend," I told Sydonie. "Not anymore."

"Yes, you are."

"No, I'm not."

"The picture he drew of you is still up in his room."

Was it? Was it, really?

"That's just because he hasn't bothered to take it down," I said. "Not because I'm his girlfriend." I turned to Claude. "It's good to meet you. I mean, we were at Tate together, but you wouldn't remember," I stumbled. "Noel told me a lot about you."

Claude smiled, but his eyes were serious. "He told me a lot about you, too."

"It's always bad when my reputation precedes me," I said, trying to laugh.

"No, no."

"Don't you live in New York?" I asked.

His face contorted. "I couldn't stay there, in the end. I–ah–I thought I could, but when the term started I couldn't go to any of my classes. You know? I kept skipping and it was wasting my parents' money and the whole thing was bad, so I'm taking a semester off."

"Oh."

"Yeah."

"Um."

Claude frowned. "You don't know what I'm talking about, do you?"

"No," I admitted.

"Oh. Well." He looked off into the distance. "I should tell you, then."

"What?"

He took a deep breath and let it out. Then he said: "My boyfriend died in a bike accident."

What?

What?

"Your boyfriend?" I said, in shock. "Booth?" The conventional words just came out of my mouth automatically, like the words Nora had said to me in the summer: "I'm so, so sorry," I said. "For your loss. When did it happen?"

"August." Sharp lines appeared on either side of Claude's mouth. "Noel didn't tell you?"

I shook my head.

Claude looked away as he spoke. His voice was strangled. "Yeah. Booth was on his bike and a car plowed into him."

Ag.

"Noel was behind him," said Claude. "He saw the whole thing. They—they told me Booth didn't suffer."

A thousand ags.

Noel had seen his friend hit by a car, right in front of him.

In front of him and there'd been nothing he could do. He'd seen his friend die.

All my problems were minuscule compared with how that would feel. How deeply that must shake a person. Just to have seen that accident, and stood over the body, knowing it was too late.

Not to have been able to save Booth.

Not to have been able to save him for Claude.

Noel wrote me those poems.

I miss you
like a limb
like a leg I've lost
in a war, maybe
in an accident, maybe
in a tragedy.

They hardly move, these clocks.
Watching the hands go round is like
watching someone's blood drip onto the street
while you wait for an ambulance
and wait
and wait
and the blessed siren does not sound.
The clocks will hardly move
and hardly move
and hardly move

He *had* told me what happened. In those poems.
And yet he hadn't told me.

He hadn't *actually told me.*

Instead, he had come home from New York wanting
to be happy. Wanting me to be the happy girl who
would convince him nothing bad had happened. That it
didn't matter about Booth. That he—Noel—was okay.

He kept saying he was fine. He kept wanting me to
act like everything was fine.

I put my hand over my mouth. "I'm so sorry," I
repeated to Claude. "I mean, I know I don't know you,

but I'm just so, so sorry. For you and for Booth and for Noel."

Claude wiped his forehead and took a swig from the water bottle in his hand. "Thank you."

"Sure."

"How odd that he didn't tell you," said Claude. "I mean, he was calling you every day."

"Until he stopped."

"He's such a strange guy sometimes, Noelie."

I tried to smile, but my face wouldn't cooperate.

"Well, if it's any consolation, Noel didn't really deal," continued Claude. "I mean, not that anyone *could* deal. It was just–I've been–" He shook his head as if to clear it. "Anyway, Noel can't stand it if I even mention Booth, or the accident. He hates to have it talked about."

"Oh."

"Yeah."

"I'm so sorry," I said again.

I couldn't stand for the conversation to go on any longer, so I turned to Sydonie and Marie, who had been running in circles around the hedge I was cutting. "Did you guys feed the llamas yet?" I said as brightly as I could.

"I want to!" cried Marie. "I'm going to give them food from my hand."

"If you go to the Family Farm area, you can buy food pellets and feed the animals," I explained to Claude.

"Come with us, Ruby!" said Sydonie. "Tell Claude the names of all the goats!"

"I can't, cutie," I told her. "I have to work."

We said our goodbyes awkwardly, and Claude led the girls off. I went on clipping the hedge.

Like a regular person.

Like a person who knew what to do with everything she knew, now.

That night Gideon took me bowling. He was down for the weekend from college, and as I laughed and chatted and rolled my orange ball down the lane, deep inside I was thinking: Are these really the only options in terms of romance?

1. Love with a brooding, confusing guy who makes me feel insecure and stops being my real live boyfriend because he is too messed up, or

2. Nonlove with a real live boyfriend who is wholesome and sweet and responsible but just isn't that exciting and kisses with too much slobber?

In other words, love and pain, or safety and boredom?

In the movies heroines often *appear* to be confronted with this choice. In actuality, however, their situations get resolved supereasily because the safe boyfriend–the #2, the husband material–turns out to be no good. Maybe he cheats, maybe he's a shallow idiot who only cares about money, maybe he's crooked or spineless. Or possibly he just rejects the heroine so she doesn't have to reject him. Then she's free to go off with the much hotter brooding guy, who magically doesn't deliver pain and heartbreak any longer but is mature and available for a serious relationship.[2]

The movies make the brooding guy the hero–the guy with problems, the guy who carries a gun, the guy with unresolved anger, the guy with a chip on his shoulder, the guy who's a vampire–and they tell you that you can have the mythical happy ending with that same brooding guy.[3]

But in reality, the brooding guy is cranky. He doesn't reply to e-mails. He doesn't call. He's only half there when you're talking to him, and he doesn't chase you when you run. You feel insecure all the time. You get needy and sad and you hate yourself for being needy.

If you don't know why he's brooding, you're shut out.[4]

And if you *do* know why he's brooding, you're still shut out.[5]

---

[2] Movies where the safe responsible guy is revealed as a jerk—thus freeing the heroine to leave him for someone more exciting: *Desperately Seeking Susan; The Wedding Singer; The Holiday; Legally Blonde; Sliding Doors; French Kiss; Bring It On; Working Girl; Sex, Lies, and Videotape; George of the Jungle.*

[3] Movies where a brooding, even sulky guy seems like a good idea for a quality boyfriend: *Twilight, 10 Things I Hate About You, Edward Scissorhands, Pump Up the Volume, Heathers* (until the end), *The Breakfast Club, The Bourne Identity, Grosse Pointe Blank, Angel Eyes, Jane Eyre, Pride and Prejudice, Beauty and the Beast, Reality Bites, Donnie Darko, Wuthering Heights, Good Will Hunting, The Piano, Rebecca, Rebel Without a Cause.*

[4] Like me, not knowing about Noel's witnessing that car accident. Not knowing Booth had died, at all.

[5] Because he's busy brooding.

Even if he shares his feelings—or overshares his feelings, like my dad—he's still not really there. He's off in his own mind, wrangling his Reginald and drooling onto the couch or sobbing into dinner or lying on the floor.

It is really, really, really not as attractive in true life as it seems in the movies.

Gideon wasn't a jerk. I had tried to find something wrong with him, I really had—but he was neither a shallow idiot nor a crooked, spineless cheater. And he seemed to really like me. What was more, he was incredibly hot and always wanted to go do fun things like bowling or wakeboarding; he was interested in school and questioned authority—and listened when I spoke.

Maybe, I thought, I should be the serious girlfriend of Gideon. Maybe, if I kept pretending to him that my home life was good, that I felt confident about college, that I was experienced in the nether regions and in possession of solid mental health—maybe if I kept pretending, bit by bit, those things would become true.

Gideon thought I was a good person with an easy life.

Maybe with him, I could be that.

In life, I told myself, if not in the movies, the nice guy should finish first. Stick with him and stay away from people who don't call you and have secrets and weird behaviors. Be with that nice guy because he is good and kind, without angsting about all the ways in which he doesn't live up to your romantic ideal.

Romantic ideals are stupid anyway.

Fact: I was lucky to have Gideon.

Fact: I was happy with Gideon.

Or almost happy.

Or something that might turn into happy.

If he could just be trained to be a better kisser.

And if I could just tell him what was really going on in my life.

The Ditz said our college application prep materials had to be in the day before Thanksgiving: practice essays, lists of potential colleges, peer and parent questionnaires.

I'd listed swimming, lacrosse, Woodland Park Zoo and the Tate Prep Charity Holiday Bake Sale (CHuBS) for my extracurricular activities. Mom laughed when I told her I'd thrown her parent questionnaire in the toilet, and filled it out again. She actually wrote some nice things about me too. That I had always been a great reader and she was proud of how much feminism I'd absorbed in American History and Politics. That she hoped I would keep studying film because she could tell how much I loved it. That she dreamed of my having a better education than she'd had.

I wrote an essay about my love-hate relationships with gardening and retro metal that was pretty amusing, if not exactly deep. I made a list of colleges with strong cinema studies and film programs, including NYU, Temple and UCLA.

When the paperwork was together, I loaded all my video footage into Dad's computer and started editing my film submission—at least a first draft of it—so I could turn it in to Dittmar.

There was Meghan, saying love "fills you up and you can't think about anything but the other person and it all seems like a dream."

Then Hutch, saying love was a reason people killed themselves.

Finn: "Love is when you give someone else the power to destroy you, and you trust them not to do it."

Mom, rudely: "That's what friendship is, Ruby. It's apologizing when you know you should."

Nora: "Love is when you have a really amazing piece of cake, and it's the very last piece, but you let him have it."

And Noel, saying: "I want *your* updates. I do. I want all your updates, Ruby." Even the boring ones, he'd said. Even the mental ones.

Plus that clip of us together when I first got my camera. Laughing. Flirting. Him kissing my neck.

I watched them over and over.

I was so happy back then.

And so was Noel.

I never thought he was the kind to shut down the way he did.

I mean, except about his asthma.

And when he was jealous of Jackson.

What I really mean is, I thought he wouldn't shut down *with me.*

Once we were together.

Because I was different.

Someone I had loved—someone I still loved—had gone through something awful. He was shattered. He needed people around. And maybe there was some way I could help.

I wanted to wrap my arms around him and listen to anything he had to say.

I–

I spent three hours editing the video of the two of us to try to show him how I felt. Maybe if he saw us together, I thought, maybe he'd remember. Maybe he'd feel something for me again.

Then I watched what I'd made and thought: If a guy I didn't like anymore gave this to me, it would make me feel completely creeped out.

I shut down iMovie.

Then I spent another hour writing Noel a long e-mail. *I ran into Claude at the zoo, and he told me about Booth and the accident, and if there's anything I can do to help, if you need an ear, blah blah blah.*

When I read it over, though, the note seemed creepy too.

If he wanted to talk to me, he would simply talk. It was useless begging him to confide in me when he hadn't even done so when we were together.

I deleted the e-mail.

Then I thought: I should make him brownies or some other deliciousness and give it to him with a very short note that says I'm sorry about Booth. That's what I would do for Nora or Meghan.

I pulled out all the cookbooks and scoured them for a recipe I could make with whatever was in the house— since at this point it was after midnight and my parents had long since gone to bed.

Sugar cookies: no.

Maybe butter lemon?

Cocoa?

What was delicious enough?

What did Noel even like?

I couldn't remember.

Did I even deserve to have him back if I couldn't remember what sweets he liked?

This line of thinking was psychotic. I put the books away. It was two in the morning, and as I ate the last of Dad's stash of spearmint jelly candies, I finally had an idea.

It wouldn't solve anything, but at least it was a start.

I called Gideon's cell phone. He picked it up before it went to voice mail and said sleepily: "Ruby? It's two a.m. Is everything okay?"

"Everything's okay," I said. "But I can't go out with you anymore."

15.

Emotional Breakdown in the Parking Lot!

Peer Questionnaire
Please fill out this form by November 22 for the peer or peers who have requested your help with their college admissions process.

Reminder: Please take your responsibilities as a peer commenter seriously. A helpful response can assist someone in finding the right college!

What are your peer's strengths?
Ruby, Ruby, Ruby. She gets so stoked about things. A camera. A film she's seen. An idea in her lit class. She waves her hands and jumps and talks, and no matter how you're feeling, you can't help but get excited about it too—whatever it is.

Also, she's amazing with animals.

Also, she is the wittiest person I know.

Also, she cares. About doing a good job. About how people feel.

What are your peer's weaknesses?
Self-loathing.

In what career do you imagine your peer excelling?
Ruby could run a bake shop. Ruby could be a zoologist. Ruby could be a swim coach or a charity fund-raiser or a cinema historian or a controversial feminist. But she wants to be a filmmaker.

And what Ruby wants, she usually gets.

I think that's what she'll be.

What does your peer do in his or her free time?
She makes films. She makes doughnuts.

She makes people laugh.

She looks after pygmy goats and potbellied pigs.

She makes the world seem shiny and sunlit.

My family survived Thanksgiving by inviting Meghan and Dr. Flack over to eat with us. It's just the two of them in that big house, and I think usually they go visit a relative, but this year they were going to be home. Meghan said they were planning to eat at a restaurant, which sounded sad to me on Thanksgiving, so I invited them.

Before dinner, we watched *Hannah and Her Sisters,* because that's the perfect Thanksgiving movie, in my opinion, and Meghan had never seen it. Dr. Flack let Dad pontificate about bonsai plants and winter blooms as he showed her through the greenhouse. My mother made the turducken, and I made a thing with butternut squash and like six pounds of cheese that I read about in a cook-book, and also a thing with green beans and almonds, so there were actual good-tasting vegetable dishes.

Dad made apple pie and wept about Grandma Suzette and pies she'd made throughout his childhood, but otherwise he kept it together. I ate a small slice of the turducken to make Mom happy.

Hanson drank from a flask and slurred his words be-fore we even got to the dessert—but we all just breathed deeply and tried to be nice to him.

There was nothing else to do, really.

Dad had a long talk with him before he left on Saturday, telling Hanson that the drinking was a serious problem and he needed to get treatment.

Hanson probably wouldn't go, Dad said.

He hadn't gone the other times they'd talked.

Sometimes, you just can't help people. You can only offer to help.

Or say you're there if they want it.

And you do that. You offer, even if it seems hope-less. Because you can't give up and do nothing.

Think how you would feel if you didn't try.

Gideon and I talked again over the holiday week-end. I called him, and when he picked up, his voice was flat. He basically grunted at me while I uttered the fol-lowing inane remarks:

1. "I'm really sorry."
2. "I don't want to hurt you."

3. "It's not you, it's me."
4. "I'm just going through a complicated time in my life."
5. "Maybe if things were different, it would have worked out between us."
6. "I hope we can still be friends."
7. "You'll make some other girl really, really happy."

I felt like a complete Neanderthal. Because even though Gideon and I hadn't been going out very long, I knew he deserved better. These were stupid clichés that had been said a hundred thousand times to a hundred thousand people being dumped, and they were completely meaningless.

I just didn't know what else to say.

I *didn't* want to hurt him.

It *wasn't* him. It *was* me.

And I did hope we'd be friends.

Though I could tell from the hard sound of his "goodbye" that we probably wouldn't be.

When I got back to school on Monday and showed up at CAP Workshop, Dittmar handed back our application packets with comments and suggestions for colleges we might like. As I flipped through my papers, reading his notes in red pen, I came across my peer questionnaire.

She cares, Noel had written. *About doing a good job. About how people feel . . . She makes the world seem shiny and sunlit.*

He wrote those things after we broke up.

Dittmar gave us the questionnaire the same day Noel and I had made that awful scene in workshop.

Noel had handed it in recently. The date said November 20.

He had written that I was witty.

That he thought I'd be a filmmaker.

That I made him feel excited and interested in the world.

As the class filed out of Dittmar's office, I tapped Noel on the shoulder.

"Hey," I said.

"Hey."

"How's it going?"

"Same old, same old."

"I. Um. I heard about Booth and the accident," I said. "I ran into Claude at the zoo."

Noel shrugged as he headed down the stairs. "Yeah, well. That was a long time ago."

"Why didn't you tell me?"

"It just happened, okay?" said Noel. "It was an accident. It was awful for my brother, but you know, I moved on. I didn't let it bother me."

"How can you say that?" I said, following him as he headed out of the math building and toward whatever class he had next. "You were behind him on your bike, weren't you?"

"Yeah. I just didn't dwell on it and fall apart like some people," he said, still moving fast. "I walked away."

"Is that what you're doing now?" I said. "You're walking away from this conversation?"

"I wanted to be happy," he nearly barked at me. "Is that such a hard thing to understand?"

"But how could you be happy? Booth died right in front of you!" I cried.

Noel winced. "Why are you bringing all this up, Ruby? It's history."

"Because you and I had something," I said, on the edge of tears. We were walking through the parking lot now. Noel headed toward his Vespa and unlocked his helmet. "We were close," I went on. "I mean, I thought we were close—but you didn't tell me this horrible, horrible thing that happened."

"I didn't tell you because I wanted to forget," said Noel. "And I still want to. Can you please just leave it alone?"

He sat on the scooter but he didn't put the helmet on.

"How can you forget that?" I said. "You can't forget that. You have to deal with it."

"Listen," said Noel. "I came back and I wanted to be with you. It was you who kept being unhappy all the time. You were always complaining that things weren't right."

"Because things were obviously not right!" I cried. "How could you not trust me enough to tell me what happened?"

"I didn't tell anyone, okay, Ruby? I didn't want to talk about it. I didn't even talk about it with my parents. Like I said, I wanted to forget."

"But I'm not a forgetting person," I said. "I'm not an ignoring person. You should have known it wouldn't work."

"What?"

"I can't forget things, or ignore them—bad things that happen," I said. "I'm a lay-it-all-out person, a dwell-on-it person, an obsess-about-it person. If I hold things in and try to forget or pretend, I become a madman and have panic attacks. I have to talk."

"Okay. That's you," said Noel, tapping his helmet with his fingers. "That's not me."

"Well, if you wanted some forget-about-it girlfriend, you should have stuck with Ariel Olivieri, or found some freshman who would think it was cool you were so emo and would never ask you anything about anything," I said heatedly. "But you picked me, and I have to understand things. It was like torture to me that you had this huge secret, even though I didn't *know* you had it, because somehow I could *feel* it there, distracting you, hurting you and—" I started crying then, and clapped my hand over my mouth.

"I didn't mean to torture you."

"I'm sorry," I said. "I'm sorry I went out on the lake with Gideon, I'm sorry I didn't know how to be there for you—"

Noel interrupted. "I didn't want anybody there for me."

"I know it's so stupid," I went on, the words gushing out. "But when I saw what you wrote on the peer questionnaire just now, I thought maybe you could love me again. I mean, not love, maybe not love, because we never said *love,* so that's not the right word, but—oh crap, all this is coming out wrong—you wrote such nice things, about me caring and about how I was witty. You said I made the world seem shiny—so I thought—I thought maybe you still felt the way I do and—"

My throat closed up and I felt so, so stupid I could barely talk. I rubbed my sleeve across my face and tried to get my breathing under control.

Then, as we stood in silence for just that quick moment, I realized I didn't have to be there anymore. I didn't have to humiliate myself this way, begging for Noel to want me again.

I could just end this horrible situation right now.

"I have to go," I said, and spun around.

"Bye."

I walked on shaky legs to the trail that led from the parking lot back to the main campus of Tate. My pack felt heavy on my shoulder.

It was only as I started down the path that I heard Noel's Vespa pull up behind me.

"Ruby," he called.

"What?" I turned. He had his helmet under his arm still, and his face was extremely pale in the cold November light. We were about six feet apart.

"*Love* was the right word," he said.

I stared at him.

"It was definitely the right word," he said. "For what we used to have."

Then he drove away.

●

"It sounds to me as if he's immature," said Doctor Z, chewing a piece of Nicorette. "And possibly limited."

"What do you mean?"

"Has he had a girlfriend before?"

I shook my head. "Not a serious one, anyway."

"He's inexperienced."

"We're seventeen. Of course we're inexperienced."

"Well," said Doctor Z. "You have more history than a lot of teenagers do in terms of having a romantic relationship that lasts more than a couple weeks."

Oh. "What do you mean, Noel is limited?"

"It sounds like there are limits to what he's willing to risk. To where he's willing to go, emotionally," said Doctor Z.

"The whole parking lot debacle was completely humiliating," I told her. "When we started talking, I meant to be sympathetic about Booth and thank him for the nice things he wrote in the peer questionnaire. But as soon as I got near him and we were talking, all these feelings started spilling out uncontrollably."

"The thing to consider," said Doctor Z, "is whether a relationship with a limited person of this type is something you want to pursue."

"The thing to consider," I said, "is why I don't seem

to be able to keep my mouth shut when it would really, really be to my advantage to do so."

                           ●

"The thing to consider," said Meghan, the next day at the B&O, "is who else you can go out with."

"What? I don't want to go out with anyone else. If I did, I wouldn't have broken up with Gideon."

"Gideon obviously wasn't doing it for you," said Meghan, licking her coffee spoon provocatively.

"Gideon is a great guy."

"Yawn. I'm sure he is. But you need to fall in love with someone other than Noel, and obviously you couldn't fall in love with Gideon."

"I think I need to be *Noboyfriend* if I can't be with Noel."

"How much fun is that?" said Meghan.

"It's not fun. It's just—" I broke off.

"He's the one you want," said Meghan. Suddenly understanding.

I nodded.

Meghan pushed her chocolate cheesecake across the table to me. I hadn't gotten paid yet for November, so I had only ordered coffee. "Here," she said.

"Don't you want it?"

"Sure I want it. I ordered it. But I'm giving it to you."

"Why?"

Meghan stood up and got me a fork. "Remember what Nora said about love? In your movie?"

"Love is when you have a really amazing piece of

cake, and it's the very last piece, but you let him have it," I said.

"So it's really amazing cake," said Meghan. "And I want you to have it."

⬤

"The thing to consider," said Nora, "is that boys are not the most important things in life." She was running the bake sale this year. Varsha from swim team and I were sitting in her kitchen, helping her make "magic cookies" for the recruiting table.

"I mean, I'm sad for Gideon that you don't want to go out with him anymore," Nora went on, "but let's face it. He'll recover. He always has one girlfriend or another."

"Uh-huh."

"And now you're free to concentrate on what's really important."

"Like what?"

"Roo!" Varsha rolled her eyes at me.

"Seriously. Like what?"

"It's senior year. Hello. College apps?" said Varsha.

"Or the bake sale—raising money for Happy Paws," said Nora.

"And sports," said Varsha. "You are like this close to being a serious contender. If you worked out more, you could get your time down."

Nora added: "Plus you'll probably make varsity goalie in lacrosse this year if you go back on the team."

I knew I was supposed to care about these things. I *did* actually care about them.

I just couldn't concentrate on them.

I still had a broken heart, I guess.

It wasn't healing, and the fact that Noel had said he loved me—all right, *used to* love me—I couldn't get it out of my head.

"I broke up with Happy, by the way," said Nora. "In case you are doubting whether I practice what I preach."

"By the way?" I squealed. "How can you just mention that as a 'by the way'? That's a serious thing."

Nora shrugged. "He's too much of a party boy. He's going to get to college and join a frat. You know he is."

I nodded. Fraternities were in Happy's future. There was no denying it.

"Now you have time to run the bake sale," I said to Nora. "Which, according to you and Varsha, is more fulfilling than having a boyfriend."

Nora laughed and ate a spoonful of cookie dough. "More filling, at least."

I said earlier that Hutch and I never spoke about Noel and me. Only now: I wrote him an e-mail explaining the whole debacle. The sordid details of the breakup, the Halloween party, the argument in the parking lot. Plus everything Claude had told me: the accident, Booth, Noel's wanting to forget.

Because Hutch is my friend.

And he's my only friend who's really and truly Noel's friend.

I needed my friends just then.

I thought maybe Hutch would freak out at the excess emotion and hysteria in my note, and do a typical guy thing and ignore it. But he didn't. He wrote back three days later.

The thing to consider, said Hutch, *is that Noel is one of the most outstanding people on the planet.*

Then, after several paragraphs about his Parisian adventures, he wrote:

P.S. After I got your note, I e-mailed DuBoise. Didn't mention Booth or Claude or you, but said (among many other things) that I heard a rumor he was going out with a sexy college vampire girl.

His reply, pasted in:

Nah. Am single.

True, did kiss a vampire at that guy Hsaio's Halloween party.

It was okay, but no repeat was necessary.

Confession: I did it to make Ruby jealous.

She was staring at me across the room and it was a doltish move but the situation was tense and I couldn't deal so I macked on the vampire.

I don't think it worked. Ruby left with Van Deusen.

I know you're going to forward this to her, so I'll just give you my permission to do it and relieve your guilt in advance.
Noel

16.

A Nighttime Escapade!

Noel,

It may have come to your attention that while I have abdicated the dubious throne of the bake sale and let Nora take the damn thing over, I am still yoked into trying to recruit the masculine contingent of Tate Prep to bake stuff for December 20.

Your chocolate croissants, though shockingly late in their delivery last year, were nevertheless enjoyed by both humans and Great Danes alike. Can you repeat the performance? Or pledge some alternate French pastry–type item?

Ruby

the above e-mail may not look like it, but it was a love letter.

Noel had made me the chocolate croissants last June—he had pledged them under serious pressure for the springtime edition of the sale, but then hadn't delivered them because we weren't speaking to each other. When he finally did bake them, it was to show me that he wanted me the way I wanted him.

Reminding him of the croissants—asking him to make them again—was asking him to start over with me.

I spent a lot of time thinking about whether to send that e-mail.

Last time we'd spoken, he and I had been yelling at each other in the parking lot.

And if Noel was immature and in denial, like Doctor Z thought, did I really want that kind of boyfriend? Shouldn't I find someone new, like Meghan said? Or just focus on my backstroke and my college apps, like Varsha and Nora advised?

No.

It might be deranged, but I still wanted Noel. Now that I knew he wasn't going out with the vampire and in fact had only kissed her to get my attention, there seemed like there might be some hope that he wanted me. Going after him might not be the smart choice, the logical choice—but it was how I felt, and Doctor Z always encouraged me to try to get what I wanted.

To feel I *deserved* to get what I wanted.

"If I don't have panic attacks and I've flushed my self-loathing down with all the poo," I said to Doctor Z, "then who am I?"

"What do you mean?"

"I've thought of myself as the girl with serious mental health issues for, like, more than a year now," I said. "So if I don't have them, what girl am I now?"

"You wonder who you are," she said.

"My point is that I think I'm over my self-loathing," I said. "I think I might actually be a functioning human at this point."

"Oh?"

"Yeah."

"You've let go of this idea of yourself as mentally ill."

"Um. Yes. I mean, I'm not saying I've handled things well or anything, but I don't think I handled them like a deranged person."

"Because you're not deranged, Ruby."

"I know," I said. "I think I actually know that. Do you know what Noel said to me once? He said: 'You're not mental. You *think* you're mental. That's a different thing.'"

"Interesting."

"I didn't know what he meant then. I thought, What's the difference? But I get it now."

Doctor Z smiled.

"It feels weird," I went on.

"How so?"

"Like I don't know what to wear if I'm sane," I said.

"What do you mean?"

"Like I've been *warped,* I've been *certifiable,* I've been *a madman*–but if those don't labels apply to me anymore, I don't know which ones do. It's like I've worn my neurotic outfit every day for so long, and if I can't wear it anymore now–I don't know what to put on."

"What's wrong with being naked?" asked Doctor Z.

●

I fine-tuned the croissant e-mail and hit Send on a Friday night after dinner in early December. I didn't want to have to look at Noel during Monday's CAP Workshop or feel his presence in the refectory, wondering if he'd read my note yet and if he'd respond. By sending it Friday night, I could be certain he'd read it over the weekend.

Turns out I didn't have to angst. Five minutes later, he wrote back:

Ruby,

I was going to say: You overestimate my baking skills.

I was going to say: I still have a scar on my hand from the last time I made croissants.

I was going to say: I'm busy trying to figure out how to get Columbia to accept me despite bad score on History AP.

I was going to say: Coach has me doing extra workouts for my knee.

I was going to say: I haven't got time.

I was going to say: Maybe I could just donate money straight to Happy Paws, instead of baking.

I was going to say: I only made those croissants to impress you, anyway, back in the day.

And then I realized: I should just say yes.

Yes. I will make chocolate croissants.
Noel

I thought about not answering him until a couple days had gone by, just to show that it didn't matter to me. Pretending that we were just talking about a bake sale contribution and nothing more.

But I don't really want to be that girl. The girl who squashes her feelings down. If there is anything I learned in therapy, it's that squashing is an excellent way to give yourself panic attacks.

So I wrote back:

I was going to act like it didn't matter much.
I was going to say, Thanks for contributing to Happy Paws.
I was going to say, Good luck with the Columbia app and the knee exercises, like we were acquaintances and I felt a mild interest in your well-being.
But I don't want to lie.
I am really, really glad you're making croissants.
Polka-dot is too.

Noel wrote:

List of things to do:
Ask Mom for recipe.
Shop for butter. (Croissants involve lots of butter.)
Shop for chocolate. (You want the chocolate kind.)

Apologize to Ruby for acting like a dolt and kissing the vampire girl in front of her. No matter how long we'd been broken up, that was a warped move and the kind of manipulative crap I usually associate with guys other than myself.

Sorry.

Mom was in the kitchen doing unspeakable things to slabs of dead pig involving the Cuisinart, a lot of garlic and pieces of washed intestine. Dad was puttering in the greenhouse listening to REO Speedwagon. Polka was thumping his tail quietly on the carpet, looking at me expectantly, hoping for his before-bed walk.

Everything was just as it had been ten minutes ago.

And everything was different.

Noel was making me croissants.

Noel had said sorry.

I wrote back:

Flour. You will need flour.

Also, I suspect, a small amount of salt.

Seconds later, his reply:

Maybe I will need help.

And I wrote:

What?

And he wrote:

Your help.

And I wrote:

My help with the croissants?

And he wrote:

Help me.

I didn't write back, because I was putting on my coat and brushing my teeth and putting on lip gloss and deodorant and grabbing the keys to the Honda and shouting to Mom that I'd be back by curfew and pushing Polka back in the front door with my foot because he wanted to go out so bad and there was no way I was taking him. Then I was in the car driving to Madrona in the chilly night.

The lights were on in Noel's kitchen. Through the windows I could see his mom and stepdad doing dishes and wiping down the countertops. The little girls' rooms in the front of the upstairs were dark, though, and Noel's lights were out as well, except for the glow from his computer monitor.

I couldn't ring the bell. Couldn't just make small talk with his parents and ask if I could come in after all this time without seeing them.

And I couldn't call. No cell.

So I scootched my bag underneath the porch and climbed the rose trellis on the side of the house up to the porch roof. I edged along it until Noel's window was in front of me, and then, feeling kind of stalkerish and dumb but also like a girl in a movie about love, I felt around for a pebble to toss at the glass.

No pebbles. I was on the roof.

I felt in the rain gutter.

Nothing but some truly disgusting sludge.

What was I thinking? Of course there were no pebbles on the roof.

I picked at the shingles, hoping a bit of one would come off in my hand.

No luck.

Aha! Tums.

I had a small roll of antacid tablets in the front pocket of my jeans, left over from the misguided ingestion of two cappuccinos in a fifteen-minute period.

I took out a Tum and threw it at Noel's window.

He didn't answer.

I threw another Tum.

And another.

And another.

Tum. Tum. Tum. Tum.

Ag. I suddenly got worried that maybe Tums were toxic to birds or squirrels and I was inadvertently poisoning the small-animal population of Madrona.

I collected as many as Tums as I could find from

where they'd fallen on the roof, then knocked on Noel's window.

Looking in, I saw he wasn't answering because he had headphones on. He was clicking back and forth between his e-mail and iTunes, tapping his fingers on the edge of his keyboard now and then.

He was wearing pajamas.

I had never seen Noel in pajamas.

Actually, they were blue and white striped pajama pants and a white T-shirt so thin and faded you could practically see through it.

I knocked harder, and he turned around.

He stared at me.

I stared at him.

He bolted out of his room.

Where had he gone?

Was he going to tell his parents I was on the roof?

No, he would never do that.

Was he angry I had come?

Was I being a stalker?

Had he left because he couldn't deal with seeing me?

Should I just go home?

Would I die trying to climb down the rose trellis?

I was turning to attempt it when Noel came back.

He was wearing jeans and waving something at me.

A toothbrush.

He opened the window, leaned out, and before I could even speak—he kissed me. His mouth was cold and minty. I kissed him back and felt dizzy and clutched the edge of the windowsill. He kept kissing me, and I kept kissing him and I was so happy. Then he climbed out the window and we sat on the porch roof with our backs against the house and he waved his toothbrush again.

"You went to brush your teeth," I said. "You kept me waiting on your roof in the cold so you could brush your teeth."

"We had scallions at dinner," Noel said.

"I thought you weren't coming back," I told him.

"I was!" he protested. "I just—I wanted to kiss you so bad as soon as I saw you, and then I thought about the scallions and I panicked. I thought, She's come all the way here and she's going to run away as soon as she smells my breath."

"I wouldn't run away from scallion breath."

"Oh, you might. This was serious."

I kissed him again. And this time I think we both felt the cold outside and how precarious it was where we were sitting. We held on to each other like we were holding on for our lives on the edge of this precipice

of the roof,

of the end of high school,

of college,

of love,

of scary, complicated, adult-type relationships—

and I felt Noel shaking and I realized he was crying. Not sobbing, but crying gently, like his eyes were leaking and he just couldn't help it.

"What's wrong?"

He swallowed. "Booth died," he said. "My friend Booth was riding ahead of me down Seventh Avenue. We were crossing Twenty-third Street and this car was making a left and I saw it coming, this blue car, and it was like slow motion, Booth crossing the path of the car and it swerving and then the bike hurtling through the air with Booth still clinging to it." Noel wiped his eyes and went on. "I threw my bike on the sidewalk and ran over. People were standing around and I suddenly realized maybe no one had called the ambulance, so I called, and I had to tell them what happened, and then it took so long for them to come."

I put my arms around him.

"He was riding ahead of me," choked Noel. "Because I asked him to. The traffic there is crazy. I just felt better with him up front, leading. But then—"

"It's not your fault."

"I had to call Claude," Noel went on. "I had to tell him what happened. He kept saying 'What?' as if he hadn't understood me. So I had to say it again and again. 'There was an accident. Booth didn't make it. There was an accident. Booth didn't make it.'

"Finally I told him he had to leave work and come home. Like giving him an order. He couldn't think clearly and it was up to me to tell him what to do. My brother walked out of the restaurant without telling anyone, still wearing his apron. Leaving his tables without their food.

"For a couple days," Noel went on, "everything was black and choked and we didn't sleep and people kept coming by. Claude kept saying, 'Where's Booth?' as if he really didn't know. I couldn't answer him. I mean, what do you say when someone asks you that?"

I shook my head.

"My mom flew out and even my dad came, our biological dad, and they tried to make me and Claude come home to Seattle, but Claude wouldn't go, so I stayed too. I mean, he's my brother and I wanted to be there for him. But once I was alone with him and all the parents left, I just shut down. It was like Claude was feeling everything and I was feeling nothing. I *wanted* to feel nothing."

"Uh-huh."

"So I kept feeling nothing and kept feeling nothing," said Noel.

"You can't feel nothing," I said. "People can't. Not really."

He leaned his head on my shoulder and wiped his face on the hem of his T-shirt. He wasn't crying any longer.

I squeezed his hand.

Then he kissed my eyelids. Kind of licked them. And if you've never had someone lick your eyelids, you should know that it's not exactly romantic and it's even a tiny bit gross, but it feels like the other person really likes you and accepts you somehow.

Like he wants your updates. Even your boring ones. Even your mental ones.

"I don't feel nothing anymore," he said.

We sat there together for a long while. Holding hands. Thinking about Booth and Claude and everything that had happened.

"Let's go inside," I told him finally.

"Yes," said Noel. "Let's go inside where it's warm."

We crawled in the window. I went first and scraped my arm.

Noel went second and said, "Why are there—what are these? Are there antacids on my windowsill? Why would there be antacids on my windowsill?" And I laughed so hard I couldn't explain properly.

Then we shut the screen.

Then we closed Noel's door.

And the rest of what happened is nobody's business but ours.

17

A Final List!

Well, not really a final list. I can't imagine I'll ever stop making lists. But a final list in this long chronicle of my therapy process, romantic debacles and friendship dramas. A list of Stuff That Happened After.

1. Mom's latest performance-art monologue—*Elaine Oliver: Meat to the Beat!*—had a three-night workshop production at the Empty Space Theatre in January.

2. Even after it opened, she continued to explore charcuterie—in other words, she continued to perpetrate creative horrors on the bodies of dead animals and then eat them—until I lost five pounds from lack of edible deliciousness at breakfast and dinner and she got reworried I was anorexic; meanwhile, Dad gained ten pounds and she new-worried he would have a coronary.

3. At this point she agreed we could have pasta or burritos or something else normal for dinner.

4. My five pounds came back, but Dad's ten stayed on.

5. Varsha and Spencer became regulars at the B&O Espresso. We'd go and meet Nora and Meghan there after swim practice. Yes, they were Future Doctors of America, but they were also seriously nice people. It was good to have a group to eat cake and try to figure out the Calc homework with.

6. It was nice to have Nora there, especially. After everything. Despite everything.

7. Robespierre got Imelda the pygmy goat pregnant. In the spring, if all goes well, two little Robespierres will be cavorting around the Family Farm. He seems exceedingly proud of his accomplishment and walks with quite a jaunty step.

8. First lacrosse team meeting: I rejoined the team. I'll be playing varsity goalie this spring.

9. Hutch returned from Paris with DVD recordings of himself fronting a retro metal cover band called Les Hommes Métallique (Metal Men). The other guys were all French high school students he hung around with.

10. It turns out that Hutch can sing–if by "sing" you mean wail and thrash around and occasionally switch into a high falsetto that makes him sound like an angry girlie opera star.

11. It is good to have him back.

12. Though now he considers himself an expert on French film and insists he is going to take *my* cinematic education in hand with a festival of his own devising entitled Les Sous-entendus des Sous-titres (The Implications of Subtitles).

13. I sent off the last of my college applications January 4. The movie, the essays, the exam scores, the transcripts, the lists of activities—it was all done.

14. Which means that next year, I will be living in some other city, learning how to make movies.

15. Though I will miss Polka-dot (a lot),

16. And I will miss my parents (a little),

17. I won't have to deal with the wenchery of Cricket and Kim.

18. And my roly-poly-slut reputation will be left behind, along with most of my self-loathing.

19. I won't have to be in the Tate Universe. Ever again.

20. And I won't be in therapy anymore either. Doctor Z says I can stop when I feel ready.

21. I asked her: What if all the panic badness comes back when I go to college? If it does, can I call you? Can we have phone therapy if I go completely mental?

22. And she said, "Of course. You can call me even if you're not having any particular challenges."

23. But she also said: "I am not worried about you, Ruby. You have come a long way."

24. And I thought: She's right.

25. As for Noel and me, part of me would like to tell you it was ride-off-into-the-sunset easy–but that wouldn't be true. He is jealous, I am needy. He is silent, I am talky. But we see each other for who we really are, I think. He picks up the phone when I call, and never checks his messages while I'm talking to him. We sit together in the refectory, no worries, no second-guessing. And we kiss. All the time. A lot.

26. Oh, and we make each other laugh.

27. And write each other silly notes.

28. And go on adventures planned by the Mutual Admiration Society.

29. And make each other laugh some more.

30. And that is saying a lot.

acknowledgments

The story about the gay penguins stealing eggs is true. It happened in Polar Land in Harbin in northern China. I combined it with a story about some German gay penguins who were given a rejected egg to raise at the Bremerhaven zoo. The panda porn is real too. I couldn't make this stuff up.

Elizabeth Kaplan represents me. Beverly Horowitz edits me. I would be lost without both of them. Melissa Sarver handles everything. The people at Random House have been spectacular, in particular but not limited to Kathy Dunn, Jessica Shoffel, Rebecca Gudelis, Chip Gibson, Tracy Lerner, Lisa McClatchy, Meg O'Brien, Wendy Louie, Lisa Nadel and Adrienne Waintraub. Diana Finch does foreign rights. Thank you!

Sarah Mlynowski offered invaluable plot advice and made me cut out the boring bits. My mom gave me ideas for Doctor Z's therapy. Libba Bray, Maureen Johnson, Scott Westerfeld, Robin Wasserman and Cassandra Clare kept me company. Heather Weston solved a major plot problem. Bob did nothing but support, support, support.

Melissa James Gibson and Zoe Jenkin helped me sort through the college application process. Melissa Clark was Seattle consultant. Mrs. Friday Next gave me the idea for the melodramatic chapter headings. My blog readers, Facebook friends and Twitter followers helped me with Roo's movie lists, swim team lingo and books for Mr. Wallace to assign. Dennis O'Brian dreamed up a meatloafery and let me steal his idea. Most of all, my family bore with me and encouraged me. Thank you.

about the author

Like Roo, e. lockhart spends her free time searching for excellent cake and making home movies. She is the author of three other books about Ruby Oliver: *The Boyfriend List, The Boy Book,* and *The Treasure Map of Boys.* She also wrote *Fly on the Wall, Dramarama,* and *How to Be Bad* (the last with Sarah Mlynowski and Lauren Myracle). Her novel *The Disreputable History of Frankie Landau-Banks* was a National Book Award finalist and a Michael L. Printz Honor Book and received a Cybils Award for Best Young Adult Fiction. Visit her at EmilyLockhart.com or check out her blog at TheBoyfriendList.com.